KANTCHIL'S LIME PIT

KANTCHIL'S
LIME PIT

AND OTHER STORIES FROM
INDONESIA  BY HAROLD
COURLANDER, WITH ILLUS-
TRATIONS BY ROBERT W. KANE

HARCOURT, BRACE AND COMPANY, NEW YORK

For Erika

CONTENTS

CONTENTS

KANTCHIL'S LIME PIT

THE ISLANDS OF INDONESIA

INDONESIA is a country of many green islands in the Pacific Ocean, almost touching the southeast tip of Asia. It is a land of forests, rice fields, and mountains.

There are large cities in Indonesia, where modern ships drop anchor to load cargoes for Europe, America, and India. In the back country are thousands of small villages where people live by farming, trading, and skilled crafts. Among them are woodcarvers, bronze-casters, and silversmiths. There are weavers, fine musicians, and the artisans that print old designs on cloth. In some of the islands the people make beautiful marionettes of wood and leather, and give puppet plays which tell the ancient legends of kings, witches, monsters, and gods.

There are also plays with human actors. Boys and girls begin when they are small to learn the history and the legends of Indonesia, and they take part with their parents in the festival dances and dramas that are given in the temples, in the courts of the rajas, and in their own villages. Small boys play in the orchestras with grown men, and work with the older people in the rice fields.

Some of the villages are remotely hidden in the mountains or the rain forests, and there the people may speak old languages and carry on old customs that are not known in the larger towns and cities.

Once not too long ago Indonesians thought of themselves as Javanese, or Balinese, or Macassarese, or Amboinese, according to the island on which their villages were built. Some of them lived under the rule of the Dutch for more than three centuries, always looking forward to the day they would again be free to govern themselves. As the time for their independence came close they discovered that they were not simply Javanese or Macassarese, but that they were all Indonesians together in a world of hope and work.

Indonesia is a new nation with an ancient history and a rich tradition of music and literature. A part of this tradition is the country's folklore, the stories and legends that are passed down from generation to generation by the village people. The stories they tell their children are old and new. They come into being in the villages themselves, or perhaps they were brought by the Malays, the Hindus, and the Moslems who migrated into the islands from the mainland. Some of the tales that are still told were carried into

4

Indonesia by the Dutch and the Portuguese. But many of the tales were already ancient before the countries of Western Europe were born.

The tales Indonesians tell their children are about wise and foolish men, about rajas and heroes, and about how customs and institutions began. There are stories about the animals of the forest, the grasslands, and the river, such as the buffalo, the tiger, and the crocodile. Most loved of all are the tales about Kantchil the tiny mouse deer who stands only one foot high. Although he is one of the smallest and most defenseless of all forest creatures, his wits bring him safely through adventures and dangers too hopeless for other animals to surmount. He is one of the heroes of the Indonesian forest.

But for centuries the people of West Sumatra have had a hero of their own, the karbau, or buffalo, in whose likeness they still build their houses. . . .

KANTCHIL'S LIME PIT

KANTCHIL the mouse deer one day was passing Farmer's house. He peeped in the door, and saw a fresh banana cake wrapped in banana leaves. He was tempted, and as Farmer and his wife were out working in the rice fields Kantchil went in and took the cake. He began to nibble. He went into the field. He opened the leaves a little and ate. As he ate he walked. He opened the leaves wider and wider and stuck his head in further and further. And suddenly, because he couldn't see where he was going, he fell into Farmer's lime pit.

He was very surprised. The pit was deep. Kantchil was a great jumper, but he couldn't jump out of the lime pit. Finally he sat down to think. As he thought, absent-mindedly he held the almost-empty banana leaf in front of him.

"Tuhan, Tuhan!" he said. "God, God!"

As he spoke, Babi the boar looked over the edge of the pit.

"Who says the name of God down there?" the boar asked.

Kantchil was looking into the open banana leaf. He moved his eyes from side to side as though he were reading.

"Hear, hear!" he read. "Tuhan has said it! Today is doomsday! Those who would survive should take refuge in the holy cave!"

"Who says today is doomsday?" Babi asked.

"Can you not hear what one reads from the holy book?" Kantchil asked petulantly. And he went on:

"On such and such a day, which is today, the world shall come to an end, and only those who stand in the sacred lime pit shall be preserved!"

"Is it really so?" Babi asked.

"Do you question the word of Tuhan the Creator?" Kantchil asked sternly.

"No, no! I shall come into the pit with you!"

"Alas, it may not be. Only the clean may come here."

"I am clean."

"No, you are always sneezing. It is not permitted to sneeze in a holy place."

"I will not sneeze, I swear!"

"It says here, in the words of Tuhan," Kantchil read from his banana leaf, "that he who sneezes must not be allowed to contaminate a holy place, and must be thrown out."

8

"I will not sneeze, I am coming down," the boar said. And he came down.

Kantchil went on reading.

Matjan the tiger looked over the edge of the pit.

"Who says the name of Tuhan down there?" he asked.

"It is doomsday!" the boar answered. "Kantchil reads it from the holy book!"

"Why do you hide here?"

And Kantchil read:

"Only those who reside in the holy cave will not be destroyed!"

"That's why we are here," the boar said.

"Ah, I will join you!" the tiger said.

"No, no, you will contaminate this sacred place!" the boar said. "You are always sneezing!"

Kantchil read from his banana leaf:

"He who sneezes in the holy place must be thrown out!"

"I will not sneeze," the tiger said, and he came down.

Kantchil went on reading. Gadja the elephant looked down.

"Who reads the holy words of Tuhan?" he asked. "And why do you sit in the lime pit?"

"Today is doomsday," the tiger and the boar replied, "and we who sit in the holy place will be saved."

"I will join you," the elephant said.

9

"No, no, you are too big, and you always sneeze!" they said. "You sneeze very much and very loud, and even a little sneeze will defile this holy place!"

"I will not sneeze. I am coming," the elephant said. And he jumped into the lime pit.

They sat together in the lime pit, while Kantchil moved his reading eyes across the banana leaf.

Suddenly he looked at Gadja the elephant.

"Get out!" he said. "You look as though you are going to sneeze."

"I am not going to sneeze!" Gadja said. "See, I stand on my trunk so that I will not sneeze!" And he stood on his trunk.

Kantchil went on reading.

"What did I hear?" he said, looking at Matjan the tiger.

"I did not sneeze! I merely sniffed!" Matjan said.

A dreamy look came into Kantchil's eyes. He suddenly clutched at his nose.

"No, no! May it not be!" he said. He struggled. And then it came: "A-tchee!"

"He has done it!" the other animals shouted. "He has defiled the holy place! He has flouted the words of Tuhan!"

And all together, in great anger, they took hold of Kantchil and threw him out of the lime pit.

THE VICTORY
OF THE BUFFALO

FOR six hundred years the people of West Sumatra have called their country Minangkabau. It means the Victory of the Buffalo. Six hundred years ago a Javanese king called Sanagara conquered all of the islands of the Indies. Only a small part of Sumatra remained free.

Raja Sanagara took his army there to subdue the people who were not yet under his domination, and he sent a messenger to the people and ordered them to surrender or be killed. The men of the countryside met to decide what to do. They said:

"If we fight, there will be a great slaughter. Many men will die, our villages will be destroyed, our families will be scattered, and after that those who are still alive will be like slaves."

They talked this way, back and forth. And then an old man said:

"We aren't strong enough to drive the enemy away

with our weapons. We must be like Kantchil the mouse deer. We must fight with our wits."

The people agreed that this was the only way. So they sent a committee of elders to negotiate with Raja Sanagara. When they arrived, one of them said:

"If we fight, many of our people and many of yours will die. This is a hard thing for our families. Instead, let us each bring a powerful karbau to the battlefield. Let the karbau fight each other. If your karbau wins, we will become your subjects. If our karbau wins, you will go away and leave us our freedom. In this way there will be no slaughter of men."

Raja Sanagara listened, and he agreed that it was better for a buffalo to die than for many men to die.

So he sent messengers everywhere to find the largest and strongest karbau in his empire. There were many rich islands under Sanagara's rule, and in them were many buffalo. The Raja's messengers went to Java and Bali, and inquired everywhere among the owners of fine cattle, and in the end they brought back the largest buffalo they could find.

The people of the villages of West Sumatra went to Sanagara's camp to see this animal. It was the strongest karbau they had ever seen. They returned to their homes and told their families about it.

"Where will we ever find a karbau strong enough to keep our freedom for us?" they asked each other. They were discouraged, because in all of their country there was no animal to match that of the enemy.

But an old man said: "Didn't we say we must live like the kantchil?" And the others said: "Yes, we must live like the kantchil." They talked this way in their meeting house. They made a plan.

They went then into their fields and took a karbau bull calf from his mother, and they brought him into the village. They fastened sharp iron points to his tiny horns, and for three days they kept him from his mother, until he became very hungry. On the third day they went to the camp of the enemy and told Raja Sanagara they were ready.

On the morning of the fourth day Sanagara's men led their great fighting karbau to the battlefield. The people of the villages came leading their bull calf. When the soldiers saw the animal the villagers had chosen they began to laugh. "Is this why we have searched all of Java, Bali, and Sumatra for a fierce fighting buffalo?" they asked one another.

The people of the villages waited until the laughing was ended.

"We are ready," they said.

So Sanagara's soldiers turned their buffalo into the field, and the villagers untied their calf and pushed him into the field also.

The bull calf stood looking across the field at the large buffalo. The large buffalo stood looking across the field at the calf.

15

The calf was very hungry. Across the field, in the distance, the large buffalo looked like his mother. The calf began to run. He ran right at Sanagara's karbau, and went under his belly and nuzzled to find milk. There was no milk, but his iron-tipped horns pierced the belly of the large karbau and wounded him so that in a few moments he fell down and died.

Raja Sanagara watched silently. When he understood what had happened he took his soldiers and went away, leaving the people of the country their freedom.

The villagers hung a garland of flowers around the neck of their little karbau and led him away to his mother.

Ever since that time the people have always built the roofs of their houses to look like buffalo horns, and they call their country by the name of Minang-kabau, the Victory of the Buffalo.

THE TIGER'S TAIL

A FARMER was coming home from his rice fields one evening. His mind wandered gently over thoughts of eating, sleeping, and playing his flute. As he walked along the trail he came to a pile of rocks. Protruding through a crack he saw a tail switching back and forth. It was a tiger's tail. It was very large.

The farmer was overcome with panic. He thought of running to the village. But then he realized the tiger was waiting for him to appear around the turn of the trail. So he dropped his sickle and seized the tiger's tail.

There was a struggle. The tiger tried to free himself. He pulled. The farmer pulled. They tugged back and forth. The tiger snarled and clawed. The farmer gasped and perspired, but he clung frantically to the tail.

While the desperate struggle was going on a monk came walking along the trail.

"Oh, Allah has sent you!" the farmer cried. "Take

my sickle from the ground and kill this fierce tiger while I hold him!"

The holy man looked at him calmly and said:

"Ah, I cannot. It is against my principles to kill."

"How can you say such a thing!" the farmer said. "If I let go this tail, which sooner or later I must do, the angry animal will turn on me and kill me!"

"I am sorry, brother," the monk said. "But my religion won't permit me to kill any living creature."

"How can you argue this way?" the farmer cried. "If you don't help me you will be the cause of my death. Isn't the life of a man worth as much as the life of a tiger?"

The monk listened thoughtfully and said calmly:

"All around us the things of the jungle kill each other, and for these things I am not responsible. I cannot take a life, it is written so."

The farmer felt his strength leaving him. The tiger's tail was slipping from his tired hands. At last he said:

"Oh, my holy, kind-hearted friend, if it is so written, it is so written! Do me then one favor. Hold this tiger's tail so that I may kill him!"

The monk looked into the sky and thought.

"Very well, there is nothing written that says I may not hold a tiger's tail."

So he came forward and took hold of the tail.

"Do you have it?" the farmer asked.

"Yes, I have it," the monk replied.

"Do you have it firmly?"

"Yes, I have it firmly."

The farmer released his hold. He wiped the sweat from his face with his head cloth. He picked up his sickle from the ground where he had dropped it. He straightened his clothes and brushed the dust from his hands. Then he started toward the village.

The tiger renewed the tug of war with great energy. The monk clung frantically to the tail. They pulled back and forth desperately.

"Kill him, kill him quickly!" the monk shouted.

The farmer continued toward the village.

"Where are you going? I can't hold on much longer!" the monk cried in alarm. "Kill him with your sickle!"

The farmer turned around placidly. His face was very peaceful.

"Oh, holy and venerable man," he said. "It was good to listen to your sacred words and to hear what is written. I have been moved by your feeling for living things. You have converted me. I now believe as you do. And as it is written, I may not kill any living creature. If you hold on with patience, other men who do not have such high ideals as we do may soon come this way and destroy the tiger for you."

And the farmer bowed and continued his way to the village.

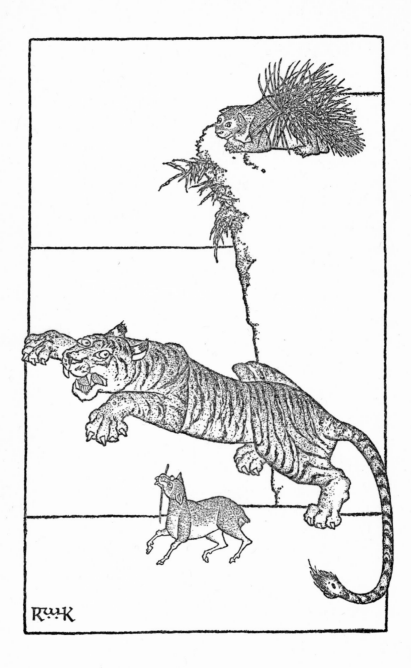

THE TIGERS' WAR
AGAINST BORNEO

ONCE, it is said, there was a famine on the island
of Java. The Raja of All Tigers called his tiger
ministers to meet with him to discuss the scarcity of
food. They came and sat before him, and he spoke:

"Day by day our food is harder to find. We are
growing thin. What can we do about this situation?"

The ministers of the tiger Raja talked anxiously,
and at last they said:

"There is no other way—we must conquer Borneo
and make the inhabitants pay tribute to us. Other-
wise we shall starve."

The Raja of All the Tigers of Java said:

"Very well. We shall send the inhabitants of
Borneo an ultimatum."

He selected three of his tiger ministers to act as
messengers, and he told them:

"Go to the Raja of Borneo. Tell him the Raja of
All the Tigers of Java commands him to send us

quantities of food and gold. If he refuses, I shall send an army against him to conquer Borneo. And to convince him, and so that he may know my strength, show him this!"

The Raja of All the Tigers of Java plucked out the longest and heaviest of his whiskers and gave it to his ministers. They took the single whisker of their Raja and began their long journey. They crossed the wide Java Sea, and at last when they were on the Island of Borneo they stopped and questioned each other. "Where will we find the Raja of this island?" But none of them knew the answer, and so they began to search. They walked this way and that in the great forest, but they met no one, for the inhabitants of the forest feared them and hid in the shadows. The tiger ministers followed first one trail and then another, until they grew tired. They asked each other again and again, "Wherever will we find the Raja of Borneo?" And when they began to feel most hopeless, they came to a small clearing in the forest. There, standing before them, was Kantchil the mouse deer.

They stopped and looked down on him, for they were large and ferocious and he was very small.

"Insignificant One," they said, "where is your king? We come from the Raja of All the Tigers of Java to demand surrender!"

"Ah!" said Kantchil. "Our king is hunting in the forest."

"Take us to him," the tigers said, "so that we may deliver the message from our invincible ruler."

Kantchil thought. Then he said:

"Oh, great messengers from the magnificent Raja of fabulous Java, rest your weary selves here in this clearing. I will carry the message for you."

"Then say these words to your king," the tigers said. "Tell him that our Raja demands gold and food. If your king does not give it, we will come with a great army of tigers and wage war upon the inhabitants of the forests of Borneo. And when you have said all this, give him this whisker which our great ruler himself plucked out of his face, so that all men might see how large and strong he is!"

Kantchil took the royal whisker respectfully. Then he turned and went into the shadows of the forest.

"Oh, what will become of Borneo now?" he said. "When tigers say food they mean meat. I am meat. If they send an army they will destroy us, and they will remain in Borneo forever."

After Kantchil had thought for a while he went to Landak, the porcupine.

"Friend," he said, "so that the tigers of Java don't come and destroy Borneo, give me one of your quills."

The porcupine took a quill from his back and gave it to Kantchil.

Kantchil returned to the clearing where the tigers waited.

"Oh, Dignified Ones, I have found our great king," he said. "He was resting from the hunt, and his servants were sharpening his claws by grinding them between two mountains. I sat before him and delivered the message with which you entrusted me. As he listened his eyes grew red with anger. At last he spoke this way:

" 'Tell the arrogant nothings from Java that I am extremely annoyed with them. I am tired of the peaceful quiet that has fallen on Borneo since my father conquered it. My soldiers burn to go into battle. Tell the insolent creature who is Raja of All the Tigers of Java we do not pay tribute, we only exact it. Tell him we choose war!' "

The tiger ministers listened with amazement as Kantchil spoke. But he wasn't yet through. He said:

"Our king in his anger plucked a whisker from his face and instructed me to give it to you."

The tiger ministers took the quill which the porcupine had given Kantchil. They looked at it in fear. For it was twenty times the thickness of their Raja's whisker.

They returned quickly across the water to Java, and then came before the Raja of All the Tigers.

"We have delivered the ultimatum, Great One,"

they said. "The miserable king of Borneo sends this answer."

And they gave him the long thick quill from the porcupine's back. The Raja took it and looked at it. A dreamy look came into his eyes.

"I have decided since you went away," he said at last, "that it is better for us to levy a tax upon the elephants of Sumatra."

And it is for this reason, because of Kantchil's message to the Raja of All the Tigers of Java, that there are no tigers anywhere in the jungles of Borneo.

THE HUNTER OF PERAK

AWANG DURAHMAN, a young hunter of
Perak, went from the village into the forest to
hunt. He took his spear in his hand and followed the
game trails among the great trees.

In the forest the air was cool, and in Awang's
mind there were daydreams. He thought of the girls
in his village. As his feet sank into the soft forest grass
he picked a white blossom from a tree and put it in
his hair. He wandered aimlessly where the game trails
led, forgetting that he had come into the forest to
hunt.

So softly did Awang Durahman walk that he
came upon Muntjac the deer asleep in the grass.
Awang came close. Still the animal slept. Awang
could almost touch him with his hand.

"What a stalker am I, Awang!" he said, resting his
spear on the ground. "Who in the country of Perak
but Awang Durahman could walk so softly?"

He took his tobacco pouch from his belt and filled

his pipe. From his pouch he took the flint to make fire. And while he made fire for his tobacco, he hung his pouch upon the antler of the sleeping animal.

He sucked in smoke from his pipe and smiled.

"How many mouths this animal will fill," he thought. "I will sell it to buy ducks. Many ducks they will be. The noise of the ducks will be everywhere. *Pak!* they will go upstream, *pak!* they will go downstream. So many ducks will eat the village rice in the fields. 'Whose ducks are these?' my angry cousins say. 'Awang's ducks!' my mother says.

"I will sell the ducks then, and buy many goats. They will eat the crops. 'Whose goats are these?' my angry cousins cry. 'Awang's goats!' my mother says.

"I will sell the goats, I think, and buy oxen then. *Boh!* low the oxen upstream, *boh!* low the oxen downstream. They trample the fields. I will sell them.

"Buffalo I will buy, much milk they will give. 'Whose milk is this?' the cousins ask. 'Awang Durahman's milk!' my mother says.

"I will sell the buffalo and buy large elephants. *Ruh!* go the elephants upstream, *ruh!* go the elephants downstream. They break the bamboo stalks, they turn over the trees. They come at night into the village and scratch their backs upon the houses. Down go the houses upstream, down go the houses downstream! 'Whose elephants are these?' 'These are the elephants of Awang Durahman!'

3 0

"I will sell these elephants, I think, to the Raja. I will take the hand of his daughter and marry her. I will buy a ship to go sailing to the eastern islands."

Awang Durahman looked dreamily at the trees of the forest, but in his mind was the sea. The forest earth under his feet was like the wooden deck of a ship. His spear hung loosely in his hand.

"There will be no more planting in the rice fields for me," he thought, "nor hunting for meat in the forest. 'What man is this?' my cousins ask. 'This man is Awang Durahman,' my mother says.

"I will take my wife and my child Hassan, and we will sail to Java and Macassar. 'Whose ship is this?' asks the sea. 'The ship of Awang Durahman!' cries young Hassan as he crawls upon the deck.

"I will play chess while young Hassan crawls about, while my wife sleeps in the shadow of the sail."

Awang Durahman's eyes were closed. He saw Hassan crawling from plank to plank. " 'Whose son is this?' 'It is Awang Durahman's son!' "

Hassan moved across the deck. He crawled to the very edge of the ship and tottered there above the water.

Awang leaped into the air.

"É! É! Watch Hassan!" he shouted. "He will fall into the sea!"

The sleeping deer sprang to his feet, Awang's tobacco pouch dangling on his antler. The spear fell from Awang's hand. The sea disappeared. Awang and Muntjac the deer stood looking at each other. Then the deer bounded into the dense brush and was gone.

"Ah!" Awang said in anger. "What a thief is Muntjac! I was rich, and now I am poor! He has taken my ship, my wife, my child, and my tobacco pouch!"

He picked up his spear from the ground and walked along the forest trail. But the air was cool, and in Awang's mind were daydreams. He sang:

" 'Whose tobacco pouch is this?' ask the trees.

" 'The pouch of Awang Durahman!' the wind replies."

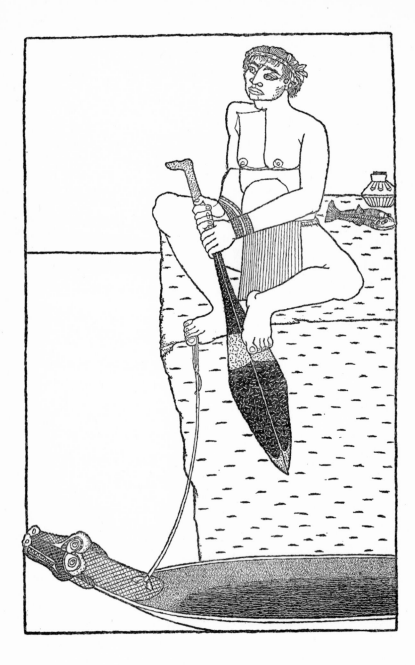

PAMUDJO'S FEAST

A MAN by the name of Pamudjo, who lived on the bank of the Malang River, heard one day that a rich neighbor upstream was giving a feast for all the people of the countryside who cared to come.

"It's a long while since I have really satisfied my hunger," Pamudjo told his wife. "You are so stingy with your cooking there is rarely enough to eat. To-day you might as well go visit your mother. I will eat with my rich friend Keromo."

"I have done nothing but wear myself out in the rice field and cook for you for a long time," the woman said. "It will be fine to have Keromo feed you." She put on her holiday clothes and left.

Pamudjo bathed and dressed in his finest sarong. Then he got into his boat and paddled upstream toward Keromo's house. He met other men in boats on the river. The people nodded and greeted each other. But when Pamudjo noticed that many of the boats were going downstream he began to wonder.

Finally, as he passed a boat going the other way, he said:

"Why are you going downstream at a time like this?"

And the man replied:

"Why, there is a feast at the house of Machmud, and the countryside is invited."

As Pamudjo paddled upstream he thought:

"Machmud! So he is giving a feast also? He is such a generous man. He does everything so lavishly. It is nice of Keromo to give a feast, but he's not nearly as generous a man as Machmud. There must be more to eat at Machmud's, I think!"

So he turned his boat around and paddled downstream, trying to overtake the people who had passed him so that he would be among the first to arrive. As he went by his own little house on the bank of the river he said: "Yes, Machmud is a man who knows how to feed his friends!"

He began to notice after a while that boats were passing him going upstream. The people were in great spirits, laughing and waving at each other.

"What is so exciting?" Pamudjo asked one of them at last.

"We are going to Keromo's!" a man shouted as his boat went by. "He is serving a cow and a calf today!" Pamudjo slowed down, but the current carried him down the river.

"A cow and a calf!" he said to himself. "That is a great mouthful for everyone! When has Machmud ever served more than a skinny cow?"

So Pamudjo turned his boat around again and paddled upstream, trying to catch the boats that had passed him. Again he saw his little house on the bank of the river. Up ahead, small in the distance, were the other boats going to Keromo's. Pamudjo was getting a little tired. A boat going downstream passed close to him, and the man in it said:

"Why do you row upstream?"

And Pamudjo replied:

"To feed myself at Keromo's great festival. Why do you row downstream, brother?"

The man shouted back:

"To eat at Machmud's house, and to receive my share of the money gifts he is passing out!"

Pamudjo thought:

"What? Machmud giving out money? Why then am I going to Keromo's?"

He quickly turned his boat around and again paddled downstream. He passed his house once more. When at last he came to Machmud's place he pulled his boat onto the beach with the other boats and hurried to Machmud's house. As he arrived, a villager said:

"Why are you late? The feast is over."

37

"Over?" Pamudjo said. "Over? And the money gifts?"

"Gone," the man said. "The money gifts have all been given out."

"Gone!" Pamudjo said. For a moment he stood silently. Then he turned and raced to the river's edge. He leaped into his boat, shoved it into the water, and paddled upstream. When he came to Keromo's landing he beached his boat and ran panting to where the people were gathered. They sat around making leisurely conversation.

"Why are you running?" a neighbor asked. "The food is finished."

Pamudjo turned around and went back to his boat. He paddled downstream slowly until he came to his house. He went inside and shouted for his wife.

"Oh, that woman! Always running off to her mother's!" he complained.

He found only a small bit of dried fish to eat. He took it and a bottle of wine out to his boat. He got into the boat and set the bottle down on the edge. When he sat down, the bottle fell into the water. Pamudjo leaped into the river to find it, but the current carried it away. He climbed back into the boat just in time to see his dog eating the last of the dried fish.

The people of Java say: This is the way it is with indecision.

HOW CELEBES GOT ITS NAME

THE island of Celebes was once called by another name. It is said that many years ago Portuguese explorers sighted the island, and they came ashore to find out where they were.

On the island they found a blacksmith working at his forge, and they asked him:

"What is the name of this island?"

But the blacksmith, who was hearing Portuguese for the first time, believed they were asking him what he was making, and he replied:

"*Sele basi*," which means an iron kris, or knife.

The Portuguese thanked him and went away. And the word they had heard, they put on their maps. And to this day the island is called Celebes.

THE DOLPHINS OF CELEBES

THE people of Celebes eat many kinds of fish from the sea, but never the dolphin. When the fishermen of the villages see a school of dolphins diving in the sea they make no effort to capture them, for the dolphin, they say, is different from all other animals. It is said that when dolphins are washed up on the beach real tears run from their eyes. Many men have seen it.

Once a Raja of the South Islands made a long sailing voyage on an affair of state to the North Islands. The wind carried the royal ship far out to sea, and then the wind stopped and the ship was becalmed.

The Raja walked impatiently from the prow to the stern, waiting for the wind to rise again. He nervously fingered the jeweled buckle on the belt around his waist. At last he stood by the edge of the ship looking in anger at the quiet water. While his fingers toyed with the buckle it suddenly slipped from his grasp and fell into the sea.

The Raja of the South Islands shouted for his slaves to come, and he ordered them into the sea to bring back his valuable ornament. One by one the slaves came to the ship's side and leaped overboard. They swam and dived, but they found nothing. They went down, they came up to breathe, and they went down again. After a long while some of them became tired and clutched at the ship's side, but the Raja said:

"Search! Search! Only when you have found the buckle may you come out!"

Night came, and the slaves still swam. When day came, still they searched. Again night came, and again day. Seven days passed this way, and the Raja's slaves still swam in the sea.

Then a wind came from the south and filled the ship's sails. The Raja ordered the crew to continue the voyage to the North Islands. As the ship began to move the Raja shouted angrily to his slaves where they swam, and cursed them.

"Never come out of the sea until my buckle is found!" he shouted, and the ship sailed away.

To this day, say the people of Celebes, the buckle has never been found. The slaves who were abandoned there at sea never came again to land. As the years passed they changed their form and became dolphins. To this day they leap and plunge in their quest. Indonesians know that dolphins once were people, and it is for this reason they are never eaten.

44

THE BET BETWEEN
MATJAN AND GADJA

‹‹‹‹‹‹‹‹‹‹‹‹‹‹‹‹‹‹‹‹‹‹‹‹‹‹‹‹

T HERE was a time long ago when many animals
who are now enemies were friends. That is the
way it was with Gadja the elephant and Matjan the
tiger. One day, in those times, Gadja and Matjan
walked together among the tall trees on the banks of
the Mandau River.

Gadja broke off small bamboo stalks and ate them,
while Matjan ate small bugs to pass the time away.
After a while the tiger looked overhead and saw Lotong the monkey swinging in the branches. Wherever they walked, Lotong came along. He chattered
and made faces until Matjan became annoyed. At
last Matjan said:

"Lotong is a nuisance. He listens to words that
aren't meant for him, and tries to join in a conversation that is none of his business. Let us see who can
drive him away. If you can do it and I fail to do it,
you can eat me. If I can do it and you fail, then I shall
eat you."

"So be it," said Gadja, thinking all the while that this was merely conversation between friends, because he ate only grass and bamboo shoots anyway. He breathed deeply, raised his trunk toward the tree-tops, and trumpeted. The leaves trembled from the blast, but Lotong had no fear of Gadja. He leaped and swung from branch to branch, chattering as before.

Then Matjan the tiger crouched as though to spring. He fixed his eyes on Lotong and roared.

Lotong knew that Matjan was a meat eater, and he became afraid. The strength went from his hands, and he fell from the branches.

Matjan turned to Gadja and said:

"I am the one who has dislodged Lotong from the tree, so, since we have agreed to it, I will eat you."

Gadja became sad. He said:

"Yes, we have agreed to it. But I must ask you, as my friend, to give me one day to say good-bye to my family."

The tiger consented, and the elephant went away to find his wife and children. Tears began to run from his eyes. When he came to the place where his family was grazing in the long grass, the children said to each other:

"When has our father ever cried like this?"

And his wife asked:

"What disaster can make an elephant give out such heartrending sobs?"

Gadja replied:

"Oh, I have done a foolish thing, but now it is too late, for I have given my word. Tomorrow I will be eaten by Matjan."

He told them how it had come about, and Gadja's family began to cry with him. All day and all night they cried. The next morning while Gadja was preparing himself to go back to meet the tiger, Kantchil the mouse deer, hearing the sound of so many sobbing elephants, came out of the brush.

"What grief can make such large creatures cry this way?" he asked.

"It is Matjan the tiger," Gadja said.

"Only one tiger?" asked Kantchil.

"I must go and be eaten," Gadja said, and he told about the contest to frighten the monkey.

"It's a small matter," Kantchil said. "Bring me some betel juice."

Gadja's wife brought betel juice. Kantchil climbed upon the elephant's back and poured the red juice on him, until it ran down and dripped off his ears.

"Now let's go to meet Matjan," he said. "When I begin to lick the betel juice on your back, cry out with pain as though you were dying."

Gadja went through the forest with Kantchil on his back. As they came to the clearing where Matjan lay in the shade patiently waiting, Kantchil began to lick the betel juice and Gadja began to run.

"I am dying!" he screamed. "This monster is eating me!"

Matjan sprang to his feet. From where he stood it was clear that a terrible thing was happening to Gadja. He could even see blood running from the elephant's head.

"Such a sight I have never seen!" Matjan said, trembling.

At this moment Kantchil shouted:

"Elephants are all right if there is nothing better, but today I am hungry for tiger meat!"

Matjan waited to hear no more. He turned and plunged into the thick foliage of the jungle. He fled through swamps and thickets, running until his tongue hung out loosely and the breath came wheezing from his mouth.

He met Orangutan the ape feeding on grubs and beetles.

"Is the forest on fire?" the ape asked. "Or is Man the hunter on your trail?"

"Oh, it is worse!" the tiger answered, his voice shaking. "A strange animal is upon Gadja's back devouring him! And by his own words he wants to eat me next!"

"What is the name of this beast that is eating Gadja?" Orangutan asked.

"Ah, I don't know! But it is a frightening sight!" Matjan said.

The ape thought to himself: "Such a creature could only be Kantchil." To the tiger he said: "Let us go together to investigate."

"I have already seen," Matjan said, "and I have heard Gadja scream with pain!"

But he went with Orangutan, and the two of them approached the clearing.

Kantchil, from where he stood on Gadja's back, saw them coming. He began to jump around fiercely, and Gadja shouted: "I am dying!"

The tiger and the ape peered through the tall grass.

"Friend Orangutan," Kantchil cried, looking directly at the ape, "every day you bring me *two* tigers to eat. Why is it today you bring only one?"

The trembling tiger turned around and fled once more into the jungle.

Since that day the elephant no longer walks with the tiger, because the tiger would have eaten him if he had dared; and the tiger pursues Orangutan because he thinks the ape tried to sell him for meat. But Gadja and Kantchil, you may see them living close by each other, like cousins.

HOW CONFUSION CAME
AMONG THE ANIMALS

IN the old days, before people now living were born,
there was no perpetual warfare among the creatures of the world as there is today. For the confusion that came among the animals, it is said the ape
was responsible.

One day while the ape roamed high on a mountain
top he looked down and saw all the animals that lived
below. He saw man working in his rice fields, the buffalo lying in the river, the tiger sleeping in the sun,
the leopard walking along a trail, the birds in their
nests, and the bees swarming around their hive.

The ape went down from the mountain to where
the leopard was, and the leopard took hold of him to
eat him.

"Why do you think of eating me?" the ape said.
"On every side there are fat cattle."

"I see no cattle, I see only you," the leopard said.

"Come with me and I will feed you on cattle," the
ape said.

He took the leopard to a flat place on the edge of a cliff, and he built a fire.

"When the fire is hot, I will cook," he said.

He put more fuel on the fire, and it grew bigger. It became hot, and the leopard backed up. The ape made the fire bigger and hotter still. This time when the leopard backed up he fell over the edge of the cliff and was killed on the rocks below.

The ape went to man and said:

"Take your skinning knife. I will show you where there is a leopard to be skinned."

The man took his knife, the ape showed him the way, and the man went out to get the leopard skin.

The ape went to the buffalo and said:

"Man has gone away, why don't you graze in his fields?" And the buffalo went into the grain fields and began to eat.

The ape went to the bees and said:

"The buffalo are eating all your grass blossoms, why don't you drive them away?"

The bees went together after the buffalo to drive them from the grass blossoms, while the ape went to man's first son who was guarding the horses and said:

"The bees are away, why don't you take their honey?"

Man's first son took his ax and went to the honey tree to cut it down.

The ape went to the crows and said:

"Man's horses are unguarded, why don't you go and feed off them?"

The crows flew down and perched on the horses' backs and pecked them, so that the horses ran in all directions.

The ape went to the monkeys and said:

"The crows are away, why don't you take their eggs?"

And the monkeys went off to take the eggs of the crows.

The ape went next to the tiger and said:

"Man's first son is chopping down the jungle, soon there will be no more trees."

"Without trees there will be no game to eat," the tiger said, and he went off after man's first son to stop him.

The ape went to man's second son and said:

"The tiger is stalking your brother."

The second son went out with his spear to kill the tiger.

The ape then set fire to the grass where the elephants were grazing. They began to run before the fire, and when the other animals saw the elephants coming at them they were frightened and scattered in all directions.

The ape then went back to his high place on the mountain and looked down. He could see man skinning the dead leopard, the buffalo eating man's grain, the bees swarming after the buffalo, man's first son chopping down the tree for honey, the crows stampeding the horses, the monkeys eating the crows' eggs, the tiger stalking man's first son, man's second son stalking the tiger, the grass burning, and the elephants running and driving the other animals before them.

And he laughed, because he saw that in one day he had brought confusion into the world.

GUNO AND KOYO

EVERYWHERE in Java, Sumatra, and Celebes the people know of two men named Guno and Koyo, and whenever they hear of them they smile. For the name Guno means "helpful," and Guno is really a very unhelpful man; and while Koyo's name means "rich," Koyo in fact never has any money at all. Whatever he manages to get his hands on, Guno the "helpful" one helps him lose.

It is said that one time Guno persuaded Koyo to go with him to rob an old Hadji. They crept in the night to the old man's house and began to dig a hole under the wall. When the hole was large enough for a man to enter, Guno crawled through. He silently gathered the valuables of the sleeping Hadji and handed them out through the hole to Koyo, who piled them neatly on the ground. As Guno prepared to go out, he saw the Hadji's colorful robe hanging on a peg. He took the robe down and dressed himself in it. He said to himself: "I will soil my new robe if I crawl out the way I came in." So, instead of going through the hole, he went to the door, unlocked it, and stepped out.

Koyo, expecting Guno to appear through the hole, was startled. Seeing the dignified robed figure coming out the door, he thought it was the Hadji, and that Guno was still inside.

"Ai! The Hadji!" Koyo screamed.

And leaving the pile of loot where he had placed it on the ground, he began to run. Guno, thinking the Hadji was behind him, hastily threw his new robe away and fled after Koyo.

Because the two of them made so much noise fleeing through the village, the neighbors were awakened, and they came out with sticks and sickles to pursue them.

Guno and Koyo ran across the open fields until they came panting to the edge of the river.

"Ah, we are lost!" Koyo groaned. "We'll either be caught and beaten or we will drown in the flooded river!"

"The river isn't flooded," Guno said helpfully.

"Indeed the river is flooded," Koyo said.

"No, it certainly is not flooded," Guno said. "If it were in flood it would be muddy and dark. But it is so clear you can almost see the bottom."

Koyo looked. It was true. Faintly in the starlight he could see the rocks in the bottom of the river.

"Well," he said nervously, "you go first and tell me how it is."

So Guno held his breath, closed his eyes, and leaped from the rocky ledge.

But the river bed was dry, there was no water in it at all, and Guno fell into the gravel and stones below.

As he lay there in great surprise, he heard Koyo shouting to him from the ledge above:

"How is it? How is it?"

Guno was embarrassed. So he began to make swimming motions with his hands and legs as he lay on the bottom of the dry river bed, and he called out:

"It's fine below, don't you see me?"

So Koyo too took a deep breath, closed his eyes, and leaped from the ledge. He landed next to Guno, sprawling in the dry river gravel.

Guno, still waving his arms as though he were swimming, turned to Koyo and said:

"You can see now that I was right. The river is *not* in flood."

The people of the village arrived on the ledge. They looked down and shouted at the two men to come out and take their punishment.

In terror, Koyo also began to make swimming motions.

The villagers, seeing Guno and Koyo swimming this way in a river that had been dry for months, put down their weapons and laughed. They couldn't bring themselves to punish the silly fugitives.

But today, whenever a person tries to get out of a predicament by a ridiculous act, someone is sure to say:

"Don't go swimming in a dry river bed."

THE MESSENGER

PEOPLE say that in the village of Selat there was a kris merchant by the name of Anak. In all the years of his life he had not been known to share his food with another person, excepting only his wife. He had never given a coin to a beggar, or lent a little rice to a neighbor for planting.

But Anak's wife, Gusti, was a woman who seemed to think that nothing could be withheld from someone in need. If a neighbor wanted rice, Gusti gave it without measuring. If beggars came to her house she gave them coins and sent them on their way with blessings and kind words.

Each time Anak heard of his wife's generosity he went into a rage. He would shout and storm, and belittle the parents who had given birth to such a simple woman. Sometimes he beat her because he couldn't think of anything unpleasant enough to say.

Gusti was a devoted wife. When Anak cursed her for her generosity she was unhappy because she had somehow failed to please her husband. Each time he abused her she cried, and then she worked all the harder to prove she was a good wife after all.

One day a thief came into the village of Selat. He mixed with the people in the market place and the fields, and he heard from them about Anak and Gusti. He decided that he would trick Anak out of some of his wealth.

He went to the merchant's house one morning when Anak was away selling knives. He sat on the ground before the door and begged Gusti for something to eat, as though he were hungry and tired. Gusti gave him a bowl of rice at once, and as he ate she said:

"Where do you come from, unlucky man?"

And he replied:

"I have walked very far, from the mountain called Gunung Agung, which is the home of those who have died. I have been sent to ask about the welfare of a man of Selat, whose name is Anak. His good parents have sent me. I am weary of walking, but I must find this man and his faithful wife before I return."

"Oh, good messenger, you have arrived!" Gusti said. "Your walking is ended, for this is the house of Anak, and I am his wife! Oh, how happy my husband will be to hear the news!"

Tears of joy came into Gusti's eyes, and she went on:

"Tell Anak's parents that everything is fine with us here! But what about them, the dear old ones? Are they well? Are they happy?"

"It is cold on the mountain Gunung Agung," the thief said, his mouth full of food, "and the old ones do not have enough clothing. As for food, they manage to find a little something now and then. . . ."

"Oh, this is heartrending!" Gusti said. "There is no need for the old ones to suffer. Anak would give them his last grain of rice!"

Gusti went into the house and gathered the finest of her own and Anak's clothes, and she gave them to the stranger for the old people. She prepared a package of food which she wrapped in banana leaves. She dug up the brass pot beneath the mat where they slept, and took from it silver coins, which she poured into a silk kerchief and gave to the stranger.

"The dear old ones!" Gusti said, tears of sympathy running down her cheeks. "If Anak were only here to bless you for your long journey!"

The thief was not yet satisfied.

"Oh, they will be happy to hear from their son and daughter this way," he said, "so they won't complain, even though they have no jewelry to wear to distinguish them from beggars."

"How thoughtless I am!" Gusti said, crying again.

She gathered up a handful of silver jewelry studded with garnets, and pressed it into the waiting hands of the stranger. By now the man was looking over his shoulder, fearing that Anak would return. So he said:

"The day grows shorter, and the journey is long, so I will leave you."

He hurried down the road, while Gusti watched him and cried with pleasure over so wonderful a happening.

The thief was not out of sight when Anak came riding his horse from the other direction. Gusti ran out to greet him.

"Oh, a messenger came from Gunung Agung, with words from your dear parents! How sad you were not here! Only a little while ago he left!"

Anak looked at his wife and groaned.

"What mischief have you done now, woman?" he asked. "What stupidity have you committed today?"

"Ah, he was so grieved not to find you!" she said. "But I gave him food, money, and clothes for the old ones."

"Where is he? Where is he?" Anak shouted violently. He drew his kris from its scabbard and whipped his horse into a gallop.

"The dear man," Gusti said to herself, watching him ride off in a fury. "He can't let the messenger go without a kind word!"

Anak soon saw the thief walking ahead down the road. Hearing Anak's horse coming after him, the thief ran to a tall tree and began to climb.

"Come down!" Anak shouted hoarsely. "Come down and be killed!"

But the thief continued to climb higher and higher in the tree.

"Where do you think you are going?" Anak cried, waving his kris in the air.

"To Gunung Agung!" the thief replied, climbing higher.

Anak jumped from his horse and began to climb after him. But when the thief could climb no higher, he suddenly threw his bundles to the ground and jumped after them. He gathered his things quickly, climbed onto Anak's horse, and rode away, leaving Anak entangled helplessly among the branches of the tree.

Quietly Anak came down. He watched the horse take the stranger around the last bend in the road, and then he saw them no more. He turned toward home, walking slowly. He was ashamed and angry. As he neared his house he began to think that he would beat his wife for all the bad things that had happened to him.

But Gusti came out to meet him. Her face was shining. She looked proudly at her husband.

"I thank the gods for giving me so good a man!"

she said. "You come without your horse, so it is clear that you gave it to the messenger for his long journey back to Gunung Agung!"

Anak looked with surprise at his wife. Then he looked at the ground. Then he looked into the sky toward the great mountain.

"Woman, what else would you expect of me?" he said at last. "After all, do messengers come from one's dead parents every day?"

GUNO'S HUNGER

GUNO, the "helpful one," went one day from his village to Macassar to sell some knives he had made. He knew he wouldn't be home again before night, so he asked his wife for six rice cakes to feed him during the day. He walked briskly toward the city, but before the sun had risen high in the sky he was already hungry.

Guno sat in the shade of a large tree and looked at his rice cakes. He knew it was too early to eat, and that he must save his food for later in the day. But he was hungry, and he argued with himself. Finally he took one cake and ate it. But he was still hungry.

"Well, I will take one more and save four for the evening," he said to himself.

He took one more. But he was still hungry. So he ate the third.

Then he stopped arguing with himself, and he ate the fourth rice cake. Then the fifth.

There was only one left. Guno looked at it longingly, for he was still hungry. At last he said:

"Ah, let the evening take care of itself!"

And he put the last cake in his mouth and ate it. When he had eaten it he discovered that he was no longer hungry. His stomach was completely satisfied.

He looked into his empty basket and said:

"Oh, how foolish I was! Now there is nothing more to eat. It was the *sixth* rice cake that stopped my hunger. If I had only eaten the sixth one first, then my selfish stomach would have stopped its complaints immediately, and I would have had five rice cakes left for the evening."

PURSUIT OF THE HADJI

ONCE in Celebes there was a battle between the Moslems and the pagans. While the battle raged, a Moslem holy man, or Hadji, was separated from his friends and found himself alone, nearly surrounded by the pagan warriors. So he turned and fled toward the hills, looking for a place of safety. The pagan warriors saw him from a distance, and they pursued him.

The Hadji went up into the hills, and he found there an old cave in the rocks. He crawled through the small opening and huddled in the darkness, his back pressed against the damp cave wall.

No sooner had he entered than Garangkang the spider began to spin a web across the opening of the cave. He spun his web rapidly.

Before long the pagan warriors came looking for the Hadji. Their trail passed before the entrance of the cave. They looked and saw the spider web across the opening.

"The Moslem did not enter here," one of them said. "For there is a spider web across the doorway."

"It is true," another said. "If a man had entered there he would have destroyed the web."

But another warrior said: "Let us find out." And he shouted: "Is there anyone there in the cave?"

The Hadji huddled silently in the cave's darkness.

Again the warrior shouted:

"Is anyone inside?"

The Hadji did not reply. And once more the warrior called out:

"If there is someone there, come out!"

The Hadji said nothing.

"There is no one there," a warrior said. "If there were someone inside he would have destroyed the spider web."

But just at that moment Tjitjak the small lizard, watching a fly caught in the spider's web, said: "Tjik!"

"Someone in the cave has spoken!" a warrior said.

"No, it is only Tjitjak the lizard," another said.

"It sounded like a Moslem," the warrior said.

"No," another replied, "it was only the voice of the lizard."

"I will find out," a warrior said. He picked up a stone and threw it into the cave. The stone struck the Hadji's mouth and knocked out two of his front teeth. But he made no sound.

"You see," one of the pagans said, "there is no one there."

So the warriors took their weapons and went away, leaving the Hadji free.

The Moslems of Celebes have never forgotten. They have never forgiven Tjitjak the lizard for nearly betraying the Hadji, and they kill lizards whenever they see them. And they have never forgotten how Garangkang the spider spun his web over the cave entrance to protect the Hadji, and they treat all spiders with courtesy and never kill them. And when a child loses his front teeth, as all children do, they say it is in memory of the Hadji's escape from the pagans.

CROCODILE'S SHARE

A JAVANESE farmer and his small son were returning to their village from the city. Night overtook them, and the farmer decided they would have to find a place to sleep. They came to a clearing on the edge of the river. The man built a small fire, and then he lay down on the ground and told his son to lie down next to him.

The boy lay down on one side of his father. Then after a few minutes he got up, went around, and lay down on the other side.

"What is the matter? Why don't you sleep?" the man asked.

"I don't like to lie on the outside, I want to lie on the inside," the boy said.

"Now that is very silly," the man said. "When there are only two people no one can lie on the inside."

"It is cold on the outside," the boy said. "I want to lie in the middle."

"Only a boy can think of such impossible things when I want to sleep!" the father groaned.

So, lying on his back, the man put the boy's head on his stomach, and then drew a blanket over them. In this way they went to sleep together.

Before long the fire died to embers, and a tiger came prowling along the river's edge. He saw the blanket and smelled the scent of man. He came closer and closer, thinking to seize the man in his sleep and eat him. But there was something strange about this creature on the ground. The smell was that of man, but the shape was unfamiliar. So the tiger crawled forward on his belly until he was very close, and then he saw what was wrong. It was indeed a man, but protruding from beneath the blanket were four legs and four arms.

Overcome with sudden fright at the sight, the tiger backed away hurriedly, down to the edge of the river. There in the water, watching him curiously, was a crocodile.

"Why are you creeping along the edge of the river?" the crocodile asked.

"If you had seen what I have seen you would be astounded," the tiger said. "I smelled a man, but when I came close to eat him I discovered he has four arms and four legs! He is a monster!"

The crocodile thought for a while.

"What you say is impossible," the crocodile said at

last. "It is obvious that two men are sleeping there."

"Do you try to tell me what I have seen?" the tiger said.

"There must be two," the crocodile said again. "There is one for you and one for me. Go back again. Take one of them and toss him quickly into the river. Call out, 'Here he comes!' and I will catch him. And then there will be only one left for you to deal with."

The tiger turned back uncertainly, crawling toward the blanket. He stopped to look. It was the same as before. Sticking out from under one end of the blanket there were four legs. On each side there were two arms. But at the other end there was a single head. The tiger trembled. He had never seen such a thing. He came closer, inch by inch, first sniffing, then looking. At last he was close enough to touch the blanket. He stretched his neck forward to sniff once more at the face of the sleeping man. As he sniffed, his whiskers tickled the man's nose. And the man sneezed, "Atchee!"

The tiger sprang back in panic.

"Here he comes!" he screamed in fear, and he turned and leaped toward the river for safety.

There the crocodile was waiting.

"Just as I told you," the crocodile said. "Anyone can tell a man when he sees one."

The tiger fell into the crocodile's open jaws, and the crocodile sank beneath the water to eat him.

8 3

THE KRIS OF ADJI SAKA

Ha Na Cha Ra Ka
Da Ta Sa Wa La
Pa Ḍa Ja Ya Nya
Ma Ga Ba Ṭa Nga

This is the alphabet of Java. But the syllables are not just the names of letters, they have a meaning. They form words:

Hana charaka,
Data sawala,
Pada jayanya,
Maga batanga.

And these words mean:

There were two messengers,
They were fighting,
They were equally powerful,
Both of them died.

It is said that long ago Java was ruled by a Raja from India named Adji Saka. A time came when Adji Saka wished to return to his home in India, and when he was about to depart from Java he gave his kris to one of his men and said:

"I am leaving this kris here as the symbol of my authority over Java. You are entrusted with it. Do not give it up to anyone but me."

Then Raja Adji Saka sailed away from Java to India.

Many years passed. One day Adji Saka remembered the kris he had left in Java, and he decided to take it back. So he selected a messenger and sent him to Java to bring his weapon home.

The messenger came to the city of the man who guarded the Raja's kris, and he said to him:

"Adji Saka has sent me to take his kris."

The guardian of the kris replied:

"Adji Saka has instructed me to give this kris only to him."

The messenger said:

"Raja Adji Saka has commanded me to receive it from you."

And the guardian of the kris said:

"I cannot give it to you, for you are not Adji Saka."

The messenger said:

"Then I must take it from you."

And the two loyal subjects of the Raja began to

8 6

fight. There was a great battle in the center of the city. They were equally strong, and they were both brave. The one fought to take what the Raja had commanded him to take, and the other fought to guard what the Raja had commanded him to guard. They received many wounds from each other, and at last, sick from loss of blood, they both fell down and died.

Today Adji Saka's kris is still in Java.

And the confusing commands of the Raja are known to every child who recites the alphabet, for it says:

> *"There were two messengers,*
> *They were fighting,*
> *They were equally powerful,*
> *Both of them died."*

WAR BETWEEN THE CROCODILES AND KANTCHIL

ONE day when Buwaya the crocodile was crawling slowly along the bank of the river in search of game, a large tree fell on him, pinning him to the ground. The crocodile made a great noise, and Karbau the buffalo came down to the river to see what was happening.

"Ai!" Buwaya said to him. "Take this tree from my back so that I can go away in peace!"

The buffalo put his horns under the tree. It was very heavy, but he moved it a little at a time until the crocodile was free.

"Thank you," the crocodile said. "Now, I feel very weak, so push me into the water."

The buffalo pushed, until the crocodile was floating.

"Further," the crocodile said, "a little further."

The buffalo pushed again, until at last he himself was standing in the deep water. At this moment

Buwaya took hold of the buffalo's leg with his teeth and pulled.

"What are you doing?" the buffalo said. "Why are you pulling me?"

"I am hungry," the crocodile said. "I must eat."

The buffalo made a great noise of protest, and Kantchil the mouse deer came down to the riverbank.

"What is the great noise?" he asked.

"This ungrateful person!" the buffalo said. "I lifted the tree from his back, or he would have died, and now for thanks he is going to eat me!"

"I was interrupted," the crocodile said. "I was just about to eat when the tree fell on me."

"I think this is a matter for legal judgment," Kantchil said thoughtfully.

"Who will be the judge?" the crocodile asked.

"I will judge," Kantchil said. "Now let us re-enact the situation so that I can see just what happened. Buwaya, take the position you had before. Karbau, come out on the land as you were."

The crocodile let go of the buffalo's leg and took his position on the water's edge by the tree, and the buffalo came out on the land.

"I don't yet understand," Kantchil said. "So that I may see the situation more clearly, the crocodile must get under the tree as the buffalo found him."

So the crocodile came closer to the tree, and the

buffalo put his horns to it and moved it once more onto the crocodile's tail.

"Is this the way it was?" Kantchil asked.

"This is the way it was," the crocodile and the buffalo replied.

"Well, in that case it is all clear now," Kantchil said solemnly to Buwaya. "The buffalo saved your life. You are an ungrateful and faithless creature. The buffalo was foolish to help you. But if he wishes, he may free you again."

"No," the buffalo said. "I withdraw from the trial. I don't wish to have any more dealings with such a person."

The crocodile thrashed about in a rage, but he couldn't free himself.

"Ai, you treacherous Kantchil!" he shouted. "In the name of all crocodiles everywhere, I declare war on you!"

"You are not in a position to declare," Kantchil said, and he went away with the buffalo, leaving Buwaya fastened under the tree.

But a day came when Kantchil smelled sweet fruit on the other side of the river. He went down to the riverbank. The smell of the sweet fruit wafted to his nose. He stepped into the shallows among the rushes. But as he did this, a crocodile who had been lying in wait roared out:

"War upon Kantchil!"

And he sprang upon the mouse deer, intending to seize him by the leg and drag him into the river. But instead of Kantchil's leg, the crocodile's teeth closed upon a tough root in the water.

"Oh! Oh!" Kantchil screamed. "You are breaking my foot!"

The crocodile pulled.

"Ai! You will drown me!" Kantchil shouted.

The crocodile pulled harder yet at the root, while Kantchil sprang out of the shallows and scampered downstream.

He came to another crossing place. He hesitated. Floating motionless offshore was a long black crocodile, looking very much like a log.

"Are you a crocodile?" Kantchil asked.

The crocodile was crafty. He didn't answer.

"Or a log?" Kantchil asked.

There was no reply.

"Well," Kantchil said, as though he were talking to himself, "if you are a crocodile you will float downriver with the current."

The crocodile didn't move.

"However," Kantchil said, "if you are a log, as you seem to be, you will float upstream."

This time the crocodile began to move slowly upstream.

"Ha!" Kantchil shouted. "Whoever heard of a log floating upstream?"

And he turned and raced again along the riverbank till he came to another crossing place. He looked closely at the water. Here and there he saw a ripple, and now and then a black crocodile nose poked out of the river. The smell of the sweet fruit came tantalizingly from the other side.

At last, in a deep and commanding voice, Kantchil shouted:

"Oh, you crocodiles, listen! Allah has commanded that today all creatures of the forest must be counted! As Allah has said it, rise from the water for the great census!"

Crocodiles everywhere in the river began to rise to the surface.

"Hear! Hear!" Kantchil cried. "Today it must be written down how many crocodiles there are in the world! Arise! Arise from the water and be counted!"

More crocodiles came to the top of the water and rested there, until the river was crowded with them.

"Do not move until the census is taken!" Kantchil said. "Do not confuse Allah's figures!"

He then leaped on the first crocodile's head.

"One, in the name of Allah!" he said.

He leaped upon the next one.

"Two, in the name of Allah!"

He counted as he jumped.

"Three, four, five, in the name of Allah!"

He bounded quickly from one crocodile to another.

"Six, seven, eight!" he called out.

"In the name of Allah!" the crocodiles replied.

"Nine, ten, eleven!" Kantchil said, leaping lightly.

"In the name of Allah!" the crocodiles chorused.

Kantchil came close to the other bank. Each time he counted, the crocodiles sang:

"In the name of Allah!"

And finally, with one more vigorous jump, Kantchil landed on dry ground.

"In the name of Allah," he said, "I declare the census completed!"

And while the crocodiles sank beneath the water, Kantchil went into the forest to eat his sweet fruit.

THE STONE CRUSHER
OF BANJANG

I N the shadow of the great mountain Marapi, on
the edge of the lake called Singkarak, there was an
old man by the name of Ismail ben Alang. Each day
as the sun rose he took his pick and his hammer and
went out to the foot of the mountain. He chipped
slabs of stone from the mountainside, and with his
hammer he crushed the stone until it was small. And
the crushed stone he put in sacks on the back of his
donkey and took to the town of Banjang to sell for
building houses or roads. Each day he had done this,
as long as people could remember.

One day Ismail ben Alang went with his crushed
stone into Banjang. The sun was hot, and Ismail was
tired. He stopped in the shade of a large mango tree
to rest, and there he met a kris maker sitting on the
ground. The kris maker was young, and when he
looked at Ismail and saw the work he was doing he
said:

"Father, you are too old for such work. This life is very hard."

And Ismail said:

"It is good to be a stone crusher. The stone crusher is the most powerful of all things."

"All things are powerful in their own way," the kris maker said. "But what is stronger than the blacksmith, the man who shapes hard steel into knives and krisses?"

"The stone crusher, he is the strongest of all," the old man said. And he went on: "Once there lived, by the edge of Lake Singkarak, at the foot of Mount Marapi, a young stone crusher. He wished for many things. He dug and crushed his stone where I myself dig, and he carried it on his donkey to Padang to sell.

"One day he went down the streets of Padang, and he looked up at the palace of the Raja. In the tower of the palace he saw the Raja and his Rani. They were dressed in fine clothes and golden ornaments, and they sat serenely playing chess together with ivory chessmen.

" 'Oh!' the stone crusher said. 'Is there anything so strong and great as a Raja? How wonderful it is! "It is your play," the Raja says softly. "Oh, no, it is your play," the Rani replies sweetly. If I could only be a Raja, there would be nothing more to want!' And suddenly, as he stood there wishing, the stone crusher became a Raja.

"He was sitting in the high tower of a magnificent palace, playing chess with ivory pieces with his beautiful Rani. 'It is your play,' he said softly to her, and sweetly she replied, 'No, it is yours.' But the sun was hot on them as they sat in the tower, and at last he said:

" 'I thought a Raja was the most powerful of all things. Why is it that the sun has the power to burn me like this? Oh, rather than this I would like to be the sun, so that I might burn the skin of Rajas!'

"And as he sat there wishing, he became the sun. He sent heat down to the earth, and everywhere that Rajas were, he burned them. 'This is good,' he said. 'I am the most powerful of all things!'

"But a cloud passed below and shut off the heat he was throwing down on the earth. 'Oh,' he said, 'a small soft cloud is stronger than I! It must be the greatest of all things. If only I were a cloud I would be happy!'

"And while he spoke he became a cloud high above the earth, and he shaded the people from the heat of the sun. But a wind came up, and it pushed him back and forth, so that he had no control over where he went.

" 'Ah!' he said bitterly. 'How powerful is the wind! It is the strongest of all things! How strange I never knew it! Of all things that exist, I would like to be only the wind!' And so he became the wind. He

99

blew the clouds in one direction and then another. He stirred up the sea and drove the rain before him. He uprooted trees and bent down the grain in the rice fields. But suddenly he came to Mount Marapi, and he could neither bend it nor break it, and it stood unaware of his fury, until at last he had to go around it to pass.

" 'A mountain is the strongest of all things!' he said sadly. 'If only I were Mount Marapi I could be happy.' And he became Mount Marapi. He stood casting his shadow on the valley, and he forced the wind to go around him, and he was contented.

"But a man came and hewed rocks from the mountain's side, and he crushed the rocks into small pieces and went away and sold them.

" 'Oh,' Mount Marapi said, 'I didn't understand. How is it a small man can crush me? He must be the most powerful of all things! I want to be only a stone crusher, nothing else!' And he became a stone crusher. He crushed his rock and carried it to Padang, where he stood in the street and watched the Raja in the tower of the palace playing chess with his Rani.

"I am old now, it is true," said Ismail ben Alang, "but a stone crusher is the most powerful of all things."

THE ONE WHO SAID TJIK

A DEER was walking quietly through the forest one day, when almost at the same moment a small lizard said "Tjik!" and a large owl said "Roo!" The deer was startled by the hooting of the owl, and he bounded into the tall grass, frightening a pheasant. The pheasant, in the excitement, flew into a hornets' nest. The hornets, aroused by the commotion, swarmed out of their hive and attacked a passing wild pig. The pig ran into the brush and stepped upon the tail of a mongoose. The mongoose, thinking he was attacked, climbed into a tree at the edge of the clearing, and in doing so he dislodged a mango, which fell upon the head of a farmer who was sleeping below.

The farmer accused the mongoose of throwing the mango on his head, but the mongoose said:

"It wasn't my fault! The pig stepped on my tail and frightened me so that I didn't know where I was going."

So the farmer then accused the pig of injuring his head, but the pig said:

"It wasn't my fault. The hornets stung me, and I ran upon the mongoose by accident."

"Then," the farmer said, "it is the hornets who are guilty."

"No," the hornets said, "the pheasant flew into our nest and we thought we were attacked."

"In that case it is the pheasant who is responsible," the farmer said.

"It was an accident," the pheasant said. "The deer sprang upon me."

"Well then, it is the deer who must be punished," the man said.

"Oh, no, I was startled by the owl," the deer said. "I was walking quietly through the forest, and he said 'Roo!' "

"Then it is clear that the owl has done this thing to me," the farmer said. "It is on the owl I must avenge myself."

But the owl spoke and said:

"Why am I guilty? I simply made the noise that I always make. But the lizard said 'Tjik!' as the deer passed through the forest."

"It is the lizard who has caused the farmer's injury!" all of the animals shouted, and together with the farmer they attacked the lizard and killed him.

THE DOG AND THE KARBAU

TWO donkeys were walking together one day, and they came to the edge of a farmer's field. In the center of the field, grazing peacefully, was a karbau. A small dog was barking ferociously at the large animal. He went from one side to the other, barking without letting up.

The karbau, chewing his cud, hardly seemed to notice the dog's presence. Now and then he lowed quietly, and then went on chewing.

As the two donkeys watched, one of them turned to the other and said:

"I am a stranger here. Who are those two animals in the field?"

The second donkey replied:

"They are a karbau and a dog."

And the first donkey said:

"I have never before seen a karbau or a dog. But the karbau talks fiercely, and the poor dog is so frightened he can hardly make a sound. I should think he would hurry away when such a fierce creature as the karbau speaks like this to him."

"No," the other donkey said, "you are a little confused. It is not the karbau who is talking with the great voice. It is the small dog. The karbau replies gently. That is the way it is. It is not always the one who gives his mouth exercise who is the strongest."

THE WOOD CARVER
OF RUTENG

IN the village of Ruteng, on the edge of the rain forest, there was once a wood carver by the name of Ali ben Yunes. He carved masks and puppets for the people of Ruteng, but like the other men of the village he worked with his buffalo in the rice fields and hunted in the forest for game.

People say that the gods must have been angry with Ali ben Yunes, for his wife was a woman who would not give him any peace. When he was standing she asked him to sit, and when he was sitting she asked him to get out of the way. If he was in the house she wanted him out, and if he was outside she demanded to know where he was. When she burned the rice, she scolded him. When he was late coming back from the fields she scolded. When he came early from the fields she complained to other women that Ali was lazy. When she arose in the morning her first words were, "Where is that man?"

Ali ben Yunes was quiet about it all. But the more he heard from his wife the more he tried to stay out of her range.

One morning he awoke early. The sky was still dark. As he lay on his mat he heard a rooster crow. And he said to himself:

"In a little while the sky will turn bright. And then my wife will wake up. She will sit up, and then she will groan: 'Where is that man?' "

Ali ben Yunes couldn't stand the thought of it. So he got up quietly. He thought he would go out to say good morning to the buffalo. He would take them to the river and bathe them. He would sing a little song to them. He would talk to the little birds that perched on the backs of the buffalo to eat the lice that hid there. On the way to the rice field he would cut a small tree with his sickle, and later when he rested in the shade he would carve a beautiful new Wayang puppet. He would stop at the house of his friend and borrow his flute, and on the way home he would play a beautiful new melody he had dreamed in the night.

It was very dark. Ali ben Yunes went out the door, and as he went he fell over his wife's pots. They made a great clatter, and his wife awoke from her sleep and sat upright, saying:

"Where is that man?"

"I am here," Ali said. "I have fallen over the pots."

"What have I done to deserve such a husband?"

the woman groaned. "The laziest man in Ruteng! Why do you stand there in the doorway like a dead tree? Don't you hear the roosters crowing? Why aren't you in the field? You and your buffalo are getting fat from laziness. Where are you going? Get me some wood! How can I cook without fuel?"

Ali said nothing. He took his ax from the house and walked out toward the forest. Suddenly he could not remember the beautiful melody he had dreamed.

As the light came into the sky Ali ben Yunes entered the forest. He heard the buffalo lowing in the village behind him, and in the trees there were sweet bird noises. He walked slowly. The sun came up in the sky. Ali followed first one trail, then another. The morning air was fresh, and the forest was still.

He came to a small clearing in the forest. Under a wild mango tree he saw two old men playing *chongkak* on a gameboard carved of sandalwood.

He greeted them by saying:

"Masters, may one watch you play *chongkak?*"

They smiled to Ali ben Yunes, but they didn't speak, because they were so absorbed in their game. So Ali squatted on the earth beside them, watching the game. First one old man would think, and after a while he would play. Then the other would think, and then he would play. And Ali would praise first one move and then another. He sat for a long while this way, as though he were seeing a Wayang play.

113

At last the *chongkak* players arose, and they went down a trail and left Ali alone in the rain forest. He arose from where he sat. His limbs were stiff from so much sitting. He looked for his ax where he had left it on the ground. The grass was very tall. He had not remembered it being so tall. But he searched until he found the ax, and he took it in his hand. It was thick with rust, and the wooden handle that had been smooth and clean was rotted and rough.

He cut some wood for fuel for his fire, and then he went out of the forest to the village. The trail was the same as always, but when he came to Ruteng he didn't recognize it. The children of the village stood and looked at him, and the dogs came and barked at his heels. When he came to where his house had stood, it wasn't there.

"Ai, I am dreaming," Ali ben Yunes said. But he looked again, and still his house was not there. He wandered down the street but the people he saw were strangers. He went to the shop of the silver-smith, but there was no silversmith there.

"Where is Achmud, the maker of silver gongs?" Ali asked.

And a young man replied:

"You must be a stranger in Ruteng, master. Achmud the silversmith lives here no more. He died long ago."

"Achmud has died? But he was so young!"

And the man said:

"No, there must be some mistake. Achmud was very old."

"I am no stranger in Ruteng," Ali said, "for my family has been here many years. Don't you know me? I am Ali ben Yunes, the maker of puppets."

The young man looked at him and said:

"I do not know you."

Ali went through the town asking:

"Where is everybody? Don't you know me? I am Ali ben Yunes the wood carver! What have you done with my house? Where is my wife? Where are my buffalo?"

The people looked at him and said nothing, because they didn't know him.

He came to the well, where many people were drawing water. He didn't know them.

"This is my village," Ali said to them. "I am Ali ben Yunes. I went into the forest for wood this morning, and now that I have come back my house is gone and the village is full of strangers. Does no one know me?"

The people looked at Ali. An old man came forward.

"I remember a man by the name of Ali ben Yunes, master. I was only a child then. It was said that he went into the forest and never returned."

Ali stood silently, holding his bundle of wood in

his arms. The people talked quietly among themselves. And then a very old woman, leaning on a stick to support her, pushed through the crowd until she came to where Ali was standing. She was so old she couldn't see well, and she put her face quite close to Ali's to look at him.

Suddenly she screamed in a voice Ali remembered:

"There is that man! It has certainly taken you a long time to get a little wood for the fire!"

And while her voice went on and on, the tears began to flow from Ali ben Yunes's eyes, for he understood what had happened.

TWO OUT OF ONE

KANTCHIL the mouse deer took his bag and went out to steal mangoes from the garden of Matjan the tiger. When he arrived he was surprised to find Matjan waiting for him.

"You have eaten enough of my mangoes," Matjan said. "Now I am going to eat you and get them back."

Kantchil and Matjan stood looking at each other. Kantchil said:

"Please, don't bother me now. The Raja has sent for me. All day I have been doing it for people, and now the Raja has heard about it."

"All day you have been doing *what?*" Matjan asked.

"Making two people out of one," Kantchil said.

"I never heard of such a thing," Matjan said. "Whoever heard of making two people out of one?"

"Everybody has heard of it, and that's why I am

so busy," Kantchil said. "Even the Raja wants me to make two of him."

"It sounds very interesting," the tiger said. "I think it would be very nice to be made two tigers."

"Well, excuse me," Kantchil said. "The Raja is waiting."

"Wait," the tiger said. "Please make me two out of one before you go."

"The Raja will be angry," Kantchil said. "But if you are quick about it . . ."

"What shall I do?" the tiger asked.

"Get in the bag," Kantchil said, and he opened the bag wide.

Matjan crawled into the bag eagerly. Kantchil tied the bag closed. Then he dragged it along the ground. As it bumped over the stones the tiger called out plaintively from inside:

"Ouch! What are you doing?"

"Making two out of one," Kantchil said. "Though sometimes it works backwards, and I make none out of one."

He dragged the bag down to the edge of the river.

"La la la!" he sang. Then he kicked the bag as hard as he could.

"Ouch!" Matjan said. "What are you doing?"

"Quiet!" Kantchil said. "Don't interrupt the operation."

And he kicked the tiger again.

"Ohhh!" the tiger said in a quiet voice.

Then Kantchil pushed the bag with the tiger in it into the river. It floated downstream. A female tiger saw it from the shore. It looked like a small buffalo, and as the female tiger was hungry she swam out and brought it back to the shore. There she discovered it was a bag. She opened it and Matjan crawled out.

"That Kantchil!" Matjan shouted. "I should have eaten him!"

"Why are you so angry?" the female tiger asked.

"He deceived me!" Matjan said. "He told me that if I went into the bag he would make two tigers out of one."

The female tiger thought for a moment. Then she said:

"How many tigers were there when you went into the bag?"

"One, of course," Matjan said petulantly. "What do you think I am?"

"Well," the female tiger said, "how many are there now?"

Matjan counted. Then, more carefully, he counted again.

"Why," he said with surprise, "there are two! Kantchil told the truth. He isn't such a bad fellow after all!"

And talking this way, the two tigers went off together into the forest.

BAJAN BUDIMAN,
THE SHARPSHOOTER

I N the country of the Batak there was once a Raja
who loved archery. Whereas other rich men spent
their idle time riding horses, or playing chess, or lis-
tening to music and watching the wrestling sport
called *pantjak*, the Raja thought of nothing but archery.

Among themselves the men of the Raja's court
liked to discuss politics, or the writings of Mohammed, but whenever the Raja appeared they quickly
changed the subject to the art of shooting with a bow.

Many young men among the Batak wished to
marry the Raja's daughter, but the Raja made it
known that he would give her only to the finest archer
in the country.

A poor man named Bajan Budiman heard the story
in the market place, and he decided that he himself
would like to marry the Raja's daughter.

First he set traps to catch wild birds. When he had

caught them he killed them, and he took each one and removed its right eye. He hung the birds on a string and carried them into the market place, calling out:

"One-eyed birds for sale!"

The people in the market place thought Bajan Budiman was simple-minded, and they paid no attention to him.

He then walked past the gates of the Raja's palace, shouting:

"Get your one-eyed birds here! Get your one-eyed birds here!"

This started the palace guards laughing, and when the Raja heard the commotion he himself came to the palace gates.

"What is the cause of all this good humor?" he asked.

"The bird hawker is the cause," they replied.

The Raja turned to look at Bajan, and he heard him cry out:

"One-eyed birds for sale! One-eyed birds!"

The Raja said to him:

"I have seen many things in my life, but this is the first time I have ever seen a man selling one-eyed birds."

"Master, they are very fresh," Bajan said. "I shot them only this morning."

"But why do you shoot only one-eyed birds?" the Raja said with amusement.

"Oh," Bajan said, "they have two eyes when they are alive, but I kill them by shooting them in the right eye."

"You are not joking with me?" the Raja said.

"See for yourself, master," Bajan said, and he showed him the birds.

The Raja was amazed. As Bajan had said, each bird was wounded in its right eye.

"Why is it I have never before heard of you?" the Raja said. "You are the greatest archer in the empire!"

"Oh, I don't know," Bajan said. "I simply do what I have to for a living."

"Not only the champion of all archers, but modest as well!" the Raja exclaimed. "It is the Prophet who has guided your footsteps to my door. It is you who will be the husband of my only daughter!"

"What!" Bajan said. "A poor and ignorant man like me? Oh, no, it is not fitting! I am not good enough!"

"It is my daughter who is fortunate to have a husband like you!" the Raja said.

"Ah, but how could I support the daughter of a Raja?" Bajan said. "I would have to send her to market to sell my one-eyed birds."

"You will sell birds no more," the Raja said. "The

champion of all archers will live with me in the palace."

And he ordered his servants to take Bajan Budiman inside the gates. They bathed him and gave him the finest clothes to wear. And on the seventh day he was married.

On that day Bajan sat with his new bride and his new father-in-law eating and drinking in the palace garden, helping to celebrate the finding of the empire's finest archer.

Finally, when they could eat no more, the Raja said to Bajan:

"And now give us all a demonstration of the strong sinew, the steady hand, and the flaming sight bestowed upon you by Allah. Shoot an arrow or two, so that other men may see what I already know to be true."

"Shoot?" Bajan said. "Oh, but I don't think I can. I didn't bring my bow."

"If with your poor bow you have achieved such honor, think what marvels you may do with the weapon of an emperor," the Raja said. He gave Bajan Budiman his own bow.

Bajan Budiman went out into the garden and placed an arrow against the string.

"Perhaps I should wait until this evening when it will be cooler," he said.

"No, people have come from everywhere to see you

shoot," the Raja said. "Show us now the skill that has brought you among us."

Bajan Budiman felt very bad. Everyone was watching him silently. Everyone was waiting. Wild birds sailed across the sky. At last Bajan drew the bowstring back as far as he could, and aimed his arrow upwards. He was terrified.

"Oh," he said to himself, "I have been married to the Raja's daughter such a short time, and now it's all over!"

He stood with his arrow pointed at the sky, the bowstring drawn, but he didn't shoot.

"The moment I let go the string it is finished," he said to himself. "I don't even know how to aim this wretched thing!"

Bajan stood as though frozen. Everyone waited. Nothing happened. Bajan looked like a statue in the garden. At last people became impatient.

"Why doesn't he shoot?" someone asked.

"Yes, why doesn't he?" another replied.

Still Bajan Budiman didn't move. He stood there with the bowstring drawn, pointing at the sky.

Then a man who stood near-by began to laugh.

"Look at the way he holds his bow! It seems as though he has never had one in his hands before!"

Other people joined in the laughing.

"Oh, it is all over now!" Budiman said. And he closed his eyes in resignation.

At this moment a young man who had wanted to marry the Raja's daughter shouted:

"This man is a faker!"

And he slapped Bajan Budiman on the back.

Bajan was so startled that he let go of the bowstring, and the arrow arched up into the air, into a flock of herons who were passing over. It struck one of the herons in the neck, and the bird fell into the garden where the people were watching. The Raja came forward to see.

"The heron has been hit in the neck," he said. "That is a great feat of marksmanship."

"Oh," Bajan Budiman said. "I have disgraced myself! Never before in my life have I hit a bird in the neck! Always it has been in the right eye! If this excitable man hadn't struck me on the back as I was about to shoot, I wouldn't now be full of shame! How will it ever be possible for me to forget the disgrace I have come to today? Never again will my eyes trust the hand that draws the bowstring! The very herons that pass overhead will carry the news that Bajan Budiman has become imperfect! Can I ever again look at my own reflection in the pool? No, no, before the Prophet himself, I swear that never again as long as I live will I, Bajan Budiman, put an arrow to a bow!"

And with tears on his cheeks, Bajan took the Raja's bow and broke it into small splinters across his knee.

NOTES ON THE STORIES

INDONESIA is the name of an area in the South Pacific that includes the Indonesian archipelago, Malaya, and various neighboring islands. Ethnologists have sometimes used the term to cover not only the Malay Peninsula, Java, Sumatra, Celebes, Borneo, New Guinea, and surrounding islands, but also the Philippines, Formosa, and a large part of Southeast Asia, including Assam and what was until recently called French Indo-China.

The stories in this book were taken from Java, Sumatra, Bali, Celebes, Lombok, and Borneo, all of them part of the modern state of Indonesia.

The earliest known inhabitants of the islands were Negritos, a small, dark people whose origins have not been established. As other peoples moved into Indonesia from the mainland, the Negritos withdrew into New Guinea, the Philippines, and other islands of the South Pacific. Malays immigrated from the continent, and they were followed by Hindus, Buddhists, and Moslems. A great Hindu empire grew up in Indonesia, and it lasted until it was displaced by Islamic political power. Today Indonesia, especially such islands as Java and Sumatra, is a stronghold of Moslem ideas and literature.

The pre-Islamic folklore of Indonesia was strongly affected by the old literature of India, which in itself had been formulated in part out of the legend and lore of Asia and the Middle East. Some of the early legends of the pre-Hindu period in Indonesia probably remain. But the preponderant part of modern Indonesian folklore is a fusion of contributions from many cultures, including those of Western Europe.

While most of Indonesia is today Moslem, certain localized areas retain specialized cultural traditions. Bali, for example, is pre-eminently Hinduistic in religion, literature, and dance. Javanese culture represents a thorough blending of the Islamic and the Hinduistic.

The stories that are told in Indonesia are of many kinds. Some are clearly Islamic in origin, some Indian, some Malay, and others may have been left by the early Negrito peoples. Some tales describe the beginnings of things, such as the sun, the land and the sea, and other natural phenomena; they are creation myths of an old order. Some tales are remolded conceptions of Islamic or Indian legends.

One ancient story says that the world was created by Tuwan Benua Koling, a demigod, who fashioned it of earth. His father, Batara Guru, hung the world (in the shape of a disk) by a silken thread to the sky. But this made the underworld dark, and Tuwan's brother, who lived there, destroyed the earth by unleashing a storm. Tuwan made the earth again, and again his brother destroyed it. Seven times the earth was made and destroyed in this way, until at last Batara Guru went down to the underworld and built a fence around the destroyer. Once more Tuwan made the earth. When the destroyer tried to break out from his prison he only shook the earth, and this shaking made the mountains and the valleys. Whenever the earth shakes, that is the destroyer in the underworld trying to free himself.

There are tales, obviously later, of how man was made. One of them says that God took clay from the earth and put it in the fire to bake. But he was very anxious, because he had never before made man, and he did not wait long enough. When he took the clay from the fire it was undercooked. It was white. So he again took clay and shaped it into the form of a man and put it into the fire. This time he waited too long, and when he took it from the fire it was black. Then he tried once more, and was very careful. This time when he took the clay from the fire it was golden brown; it was the Indonesian.

The stories Indonesians tell explain many things—why Moslems kill lizards and not spiders, why children lose their front teeth, why bridegrooms wear garlands of flowers around their krisses, why mothers carry crying babies outside the house to make them stop crying, why a man should not intrude himself in the cooking of rice, how Celebes, Minangkabau and other places got their names, why the rooster crows, why the original inhabitants of Indonesia have curly hair, and why the people of Celebes will not eat dolphins.

Some of the stories have moral meanings. Some are philosophic. And some are sheer humor.

There are many legends of a more or less contemporary feeling. One of them recounts how a Portuguese engineer attempted to build a canal across a peninsula of the island of Amboina. The Amboinese held that the ground through which the canal was to go was sacred, and they refused to help. The Portuguese imported Javanese laborers for the work. At the crucial point of the construction, the Portuguese engineer set off a dynamite blast. Water came to the surface. A second dynamite blast brought blood to the surface. And on the third blast, the removed dirt of its own accord filled up the excavation.

Another "modern" legend of this type comes from the Moluccas. It tells why Saparua is in reality only half an island. When the people of the eastern end and the western end could not get along together, the island finally broke in half, and one end floated away. The people of the two half-islands are said to be related, but one group is Moslem and the other Christian.

A similar legend explains how Java and Bali became separated. It is said that they were once joined together by a narrow isthmus. A Raja of Java, after having banished his son to the Balinese end of the single island, drew a line with his finger across the sands of the isthmus to dramatize his action. The water from both sides flowed together there, and the single island became two.

There is a cycle of tales about Abu Nawas (or Nuwas), the Islamic comedy hero who is always outwitting royalty. He is known not only in Indonesia but elsewhere in the Moslem world. Abu Nawas was actually a Persian poet of the Middle Ages. Many incidents and episodes have been attached to his name much as many favorite American stories have been attributed to Lincoln. Another Indonesian character who appears frequently in the tales is Bajan Budiman. His adventures are of the same variety as those of Abu Nawas; he is always testing his wits against those of the Raja.

Animal stories too are much loved by Indonesians. The hero of the forest is Kantchil, the mouse deer, who stands less than a foot high. Cleverer than all other animals (and sometimes cleverer than man),

Kantchil (also called Pelanduk) continually provokes and then outwits such creatures as the tiger, the crocodile, the elephant, the buffalo, and the hyena. His adventures have an almost universal character. Some of the stories are similar to the American Brer Rabbit tales, and to the Anansi tales of West Africa. But Kantchil has a personality which is uniquely Indonesian.

All of the stories in this book have been recorded from verbal narrations by people from Sumatra, Java, Celebes, and Lombok. Some are widely known, some only locally. This book does not contain examples of mythology, original creation tales, or epic adventures of gods and demigods. Its intention is to present what might be called "living folklore." The feeling is contemporary rather than classical in spirit. Some of the stories are uncontestably old, but they are related to a background of modern Indonesia. Some are not so much "stories" as anecdotes or explanations, but they are imaginative reflections upon phenomena, institutions, mores, and foibles of the people.

Many thanks are due to the friends who assisted in the collection of the tales from which the twenty-three examples in this book have been selected. I am especially grateful to Sulin ben Ismail, Kahrudin Younes, Raden Suwanto, Machmud Raksapermana, and Ahmat Shamsul.

KANTCHIL'S LIME PIT (from Java, Sumatra, Celebes, Malaya): Kantchil the mouse deer (also known as Pelanduk) is the main hero-trickster of Indonesian folklore. In some local areas the trickster part is taken by the ape, and even less frequently, by the tortoise. Kantchil's adventures are known as far north as the Philippines and also on the mainland in Malaya and Indo-China. There is a cunning sharpness and at the same time a humorous pomposity in Kantchil's character which gives no end of delight to Indonesian children. In almost every instance Kantchil emerges the victor against the larger beasts of the forest. Most frequently it is the tiger who is the antagonist and the victim, sometimes the elephant or the crocodile. Other animals also come in for their turn. In a very few tales Kantchil himself is the victim. His conqueror, however, is a still smaller animal, such as the crab. In one instance Kantchil runs a race with, as he thinks, one crab; but each time he comes to a turn in the race around the lake another crab pops out of its hole and says, "Here I am!" This story, of course, is widely known, with different actors, around the world. Following this episode, however, Kantchil avenges himself on the crabs by getting the elephant to trample on their houses. In the Lime Pit story, Kantchil quotes God as he spins his plot; in other tales he variously calls upon Mohammed and the Raja to support his wisdom and authority. One of Kantchil's adventures involves the familiar "tar-baby" incident. In its general lines it is very similar to the American Negro Brer Rabbit variant.

THE VICTORY OF THE BUFFALO (from Java, Sumatra): This is a "how it came about" story. The legendary battle of the buffalo is supposed to have taken place during the Majapahit Empire period, about the 13th century A.D. Under Dutch rule, Minangkabau was officially called simply West Sumatra, or Sumatra Barat, but local inhabitants preferred the old name of the area. It is said that the exact place where the famous battle took place is still pointed out to visitors.

THE TIGER'S TAIL (from Sumatra): Known also in Korea and China, this story is a commentary on hypocrisy. It reflects on moral attitudes which are frequently taken by people who do not have to face real life situations.

THE TIGERS' WAR AGAINST BORNEO (from Java): The theme of this story is based upon a zoological reality. There are no tigers in Borneo. The flora and fauna of Java and Sumatra are similar to those of the mainland, but Borneo shows every indication of having been separated from the mainland at a very early geological period. This tale, like many others, contains the explanation of an observable fact, and it is the wise Kantchil who is credited with keeping the tigers out of Borneo.

THE HUNTER OF PERAK (from Java, Sumatra, Malaya): Variants of this story are known throughout the archipelago and on the Asiatic mainland. The basic idea—of "counting chickens before they are hatched" —is common to most folk cultures around the world. Special localized variants appear in Europe, Haiti, India, and Korea, to name only a few areas where the theme exists. Compare, for example, "Uncle Bouqui Buys a Burro" in Courlander, *Uncle Bouqui of Haiti* (New York, Holt, 1942) with "The Daydreamer" in C. H. Bompas, *Folklore of the Santal Parganas* (London, D. Nutt, 1909). An old Indian version of the story is found in the *Panchatantra*. "The Hunter of Perak" as given in this present collection is actually a synthesis of three Indonesian variants. Two of them, from Java and Sumatra, were given by Indonesian informants; the third, a Malayan version, was heard by I. H. N. Evans and published in his *Studies in Religion, Folklore, and Custom in North Borneo and the Malay Peninsula* (London, Cambridge, 1923). The name of the hunter is taken from the Evans variant.

PAMUDJO'S FEAST (from Java): Besides demonstrating an epigram, this tale illustrates the institution of *sadakah,* the giving of money gifts. When a rich man gives a feast he invites special guests, but the poorer of his neighbors may attend without invitation. On some occasions the climax of the feast is when the host passes out money gifts to those attending.

HOW CELEBES GOT ITS NAME (from Celebes and Lombok): Many of the "how it began" stories of Indonesia explain the origin of place names in this way.

THE DOLPHINS OF CELEBES (from Celebes): Another story explaining origins, this piece has some of the quality of mythology and a strong poetic feeling that is encountered frequently in Indonesian folklore. The "North Islands" referred to are probably the Philippines, which at an early date were part of the aboriginal culture area of Indonesia. Some of the older Indonesian legends are known in the Philippines, and the Negrito racial stocks of both island groups are closely related.

THE BET BETWEEN MATJAN AND GADJA (from Sumatra, Malaya, Java): A number of variants of this tale are dispersed throughout the main Indonesian islands, as well as on the Malay Peninsula. In one variant it is molasses that Kantchil pours on the elephant's back, rather than betel juice. In others, the ape and the tiger tie their tails together, and the ape rides the tiger back through the grass to size up the situation that has frightened Matjan; when Kantchil frightens the tiger a second time, he flees through the forest dragging the ape after him, and the ape dies of the rough treatment. The theme of tying the tails together is known elsewhere in oriental lore. One example is the Ethiopian tale in which the small monkey sews the tail of the ape to that of a dead leopard; the leopard is suddenly uncovered, and the ape flees, dragging the corpse after him. The orangutan, the most manlike of apes in Indonesia, is rarely encountered in folklore. Usually it is the white ape (Celebes) or the black ape (Sumatra) who appears. The word *oran* means man in Malayu. *Oran Blanda,* for example, means Dutchman; *Oran Puti* means white man; the people at the westernmost part of Java are called *Oran Badue;* people in middle eastern Java are called *Oran Tenger,* or mountain people. And *orangutan,* the name of the ape in this story, means "man of the forest," or "wild man."

HOW CONFUSION CAME AMONG THE ANIMALS (from Celebes): In this story the ape, rather than Kantchil, is the trickster. The story differs from the usual run of Kantchil's adventures in that the ape's sport is a little on the malevolent side, and his actions are humorless and pointless. There is almost always a raison d'être in Kantchil's behavior, and none at all in this escapade of the ape. However, the panoramic scope of his drama is Wagnerian in conception. Sitting on his mountain top, looking in all directions to see the damage he has wrought and the chain reaction of evil, the ape is a symbol of badness. There are several known Asiatic variants of this theme.

GUNO AND KOYO (from Sumatra): Guno and Koyo are a team of comic characters well-known in Indonesian lore. Guno's name in Malayu means "useful" or "helpful," and he is always the contrary of useful or helpful. Koyo means "wealth," and the character by this name always manages to lose everything, usually with Guno's aid. Their behavior follows strictly low comedy lines.

THE MESSENGER (from Bali): The mountain Gunung Agung in Bali is a sacred place, being one of four great peaks said to have been constructed by the Hindu gods when they moved to this island. Gunung Agung is the highest of the peaks, and is supposed to be the navel of the world. It occupies a role in legend similar to that of Mount Kailasa in India. In the old lore of the Nabaloi people of the Philippines, Mount Pulag has the same mythological associations. A huge temple is built on the side of Bali's Gunung Agung, about halfway up the slope. Whether the idea of the dead going to reside on the mountain is part of a well-

NOTES ON THE STORIES

defined mythology or not is not clear. Indian informants have stated that the tale is known in both north
and south India.

GUNO'S HUNGER (from Sumatra): This little episode
is one of many of the silly predicaments Guno—gen-
erally in the company of Koyo—gets into. A similar
tale of the foolish man is known in north India.

PURSUIT OF THE HADJI (from South Celebes): This
story, in which the central figure is a Hadji (a Moslem who has made the pilgrimage to Mecca), is
clearly based on ancient Moslem lore. Moslem tradition recounts that the Prophet Mohammed, after a
visit to Mecca, was pursued by enemies, and he took
refuge in a cave; the spider, as in this story, spun a
protective web across the entrance and saved Mohammed from death. But the theme is still older. The
Jewish David, seeking refuge from King Saul who
had sent soldiers to kill him, entered a cave and was
in the same way saved by the spider.

CROCODILE'S SHARE (from Sumatra, Java): As in
many other Indonesian stories, the tiger, king of
beasts, is easily upset by strange phenomena. In "The
Bet Between Matjan and Gadja" it is the sight of the
tiny mouse deer "eating" the elephant which upsets
him; here it is a body that smells human but seems to

have four arms and legs. And as in many other tales, the tiger has to be urged on, and ends up as the victim.

THE KRIS OF ADJI SAKA (from Java): On learning this quatrain, which is both simple and dramatic, Javanese children have immediately acquired the "naked alphabet" of Java—that is, the fundamental letters without special vowel values. When vowel values are added by small marks near the "naked" characters, the letters are called "clothed."

WAR BETWEEN THE CROCODILES AND KANTCHIL (from Java, Sumatra, Malaya): The four incidents included here in the feud between the crocodiles and Kantchil represent only a portion of a Kantchil cycle in which the mouse deer goes out of his way to provoke, and then outwits, many animals of the forest. Some of the episodes, very brief in content, tell how Kantchil, pursued by the tiger, gets that animal to beat on the Raja's (in some versions, Mohammed's) drum, which is in reality a wasps' nest; how he gets the tiger to listen to the Raja's music by putting his ear (sometimes his tongue) between two large bamboo stalks, where it is pinched; how he gives the tiger the Raja's belt (in some versions Solomon's turban) to put on—in reality a coiled snake; and so on. One incident follows upon the other in an endless sequence, and the episodes are put together in various combinations by the individual story tellers. As narrated here, Kantchil in a very simple way gets the buffalo out of the crocodile's clutches. In some Indonesian variants it is a man who saves the crocodile, and whom the crocodile wishes to eat. The man calls upon objects floating down the river to judge as to the justice of the crocodile's claim on him. An old plate, the limb of a tree, an old grass mat, each in turn is disgruntled with the way man has treated it in its old age, and therefore judges in favor of the crocodile, until at last Kantchil saves the day. This somewhat more philosophical treatment has close parallels in Somaliland, Ethiopia, elsewhere in East Africa, northeast India, and in Arabia. In one Indonesian variant, as in the Ethiopian account, a snake is the villain.

THE STONE CRUSHER OF BANJANG (from Sumatra): Another Indonesian variant of this tale tells how a rat went out to marry into the most powerful of all families, beginning with that of God; he ends up by marrying another rat who digs holes in the side of the mountain. The theme is familiar in Ethiopia, elsewhere in East Africa, in Korea, in Japan, and in other parts of East Asia. In almost identical form it appears as one of the tales in India's classical *Panchatantra*.

THE ONE WHO SAID TJIK (from Borneo): This story, with varying casts of characters, is known throughout Indonesia, as well as in Indo-China and the Philippines. Its moral observation, that the small and weak are sometimes punished for the crimes of the strong, recalls a similar Ethiopian folktale in which the herbiverous donkey is punished for the sin of eating a blade of grass, while the lion and the hyena, who kill to eat, act as the jury. Still another Ethiopian tale recounts how the leopard, on learning that his son has been killed by an elephant, goes out and slaughters goats in revenge.

THE DOG AND THE KARBAU (from Borneo): This short tale has a calm reflective tone and an implicit moral. It comments graphically upon human behavior and points out that violent speech is the recourse of those who feel weaker than others. In one Javanese variant, instead of two donkeys it is a Javanese and a near-sighted Dutchman who observe the dog and the karbau. The theme is known elsewhere in the islands, including the Philippines and New Guinea.

THE WOOD CARVER OF RUTENG (from Sumatra): The story of the telescoping of time is a familiar theme in the lore of both Asia and Europe. The Dutch-American legend of Rip Van Winkle is a close parallel of this tale. One may guess that the Indonesian variant might have had a European origin, although it has a flavor which is distinctly a local one. The game *chongkak,* or *main chongkak,* is known throughout Indonesia. It is played on a board with sixteen pockets or holes, in two rows of eight. The playing pieces are usually seeds or beans. The same game, with local variations, is known throughout Africa under the names *bwari, mungala, gebeta,* etc. In another Indonesian version, the men in the forest are playing chess. The Wayang referred to in the story is a typical Indonesian drama. It is sometimes performed by human actors, sometimes by puppets, always to the accompaniment of music. Ali addresses the men in the forest by the title "Master" (*Tuan*) as a sign of respect. Young people in Java and Sumatra use this term in speaking to older men. Although Ali's physical appearance upon his return from the forest is not described, it can be inferred from the fact that the villagers address him as "Master." Several stories with themes somewhat similar to this one are known in Japan, Korea, and India.

TWO OUT OF ONE (from Malaya and the Philippines): This tale about Kantchil's outwitting of the tiger has an unusually imaginative quality. The idea of making two people out of one, and two tigers out of one, fascinates not only Matjan, but the Indonesian children as well. A variant is known in northeastern India. (See: C. H. Bompas, *Folklore of the Santal Parganas.*)

BAJAN BUDIMAN, THE SHARPSHOOTER (from Sumatra): The adventure Bajan Budiman goes through in this tale is elsewhere attributed to Abu Nuwas, the Islamic comic hero. The use of the bow and arrow is rather ancient and classical in Indonesian culture. Although this weapon was once common for the hunting of animals, it now survives mostly in memory, through the classical dance dramas of Sumatra, Java, and Bali. One of the Budiman tales tells how Budiman and another man work as laborers in a mosque. Both live equal distances away, Budiman five miles to the west of the mosque, the other man five miles to the east. When the work is over, Budiman demands more pay than the other laborer. Officials of the mosque cite geography to prove both men must walk the same distance. But Budiman points out that his face is badly burned by the sun, since he has to walk into the sun each morning and each evening, and he wins his point.

GLOSSARY AND
PRONUNCIATION GUIDE

Abu Nawas (ah-boo nah-wahss), Abu Nuwas (ah-boo noo-wahss)—An Islamic folklore hero.

Adji Saka (ahd-jee sah-kah)—The name of a legendary Indian price.

Ali ben Yunes (ah-lee behn yoo-nehss)—A man's name.

Allah (ah-lah)—The Islamic name for God.

Amboina (ahm-boy-nah)—One of the islands of the United States of Indonesia.

Annam (ah-nahm)—A French-controlled state in Southeast Asia.

Awang Durahman (ah-wahng doo-rah-mahn)—A man's name.

Babi (bah-bee)—The boar, or pig.

Bajan Budiman (bah-yahn boo-dee-mahn)—The name of a comic folklore hero.

Bali (bah-lee)—One of the islands of Indonesia.

Banjang (bahn-jahng)—A small Indonesian town.

Batak (bah-tahk)—One of the cultural groups of Sumatra. Also, loosely, an area.

Batara Guru (bah-tah-rah goo-roo)—An Indonesian demi-god who played a part in the creation of the world.

Betel (bee-t'l)—The name of a certain type of palm tree, the fruit of which are called betel nuts.

Borneo (bohr-nee-oh)—One of the main Indonesian islands.

Buwaya (boo-wah-yah)—The crocodile.

Chongkak (chong-kahk)—An Indonesian game played on a board or tray with seeds.

Celebes (seh-leh-behss)—One of the main islands of Indonesia.

Gadja (gahd-jah)—The elephant.

Garangkang (gah-rahng-kahng)—The spider.

Guno (goo-no)—An Indonesian folklore comedy character.

Gunung Agung (goo-noong ah-goong)—A mountain in Bali.

Hadji (hahd-jee)—A Moslem who has made the pilgrimage to Mecca.

Hassan (hah-sahn)—a man's name.

Hindu (hihn-doo)—A member of the religious faith known as Hinduism. Also refers to the culture of Hindu areas of India.

Indo-China—A French-controlled area in Southeast Asia.

Islam (ihs-lahm)—The Moslem religion. More broadly, the Moslem culture area.

Ismail ben Alang (ihs-myl behn ah-lahng)—A man's name.

Java (jah-vah)—One of the main islands of Indonesia.

Karbau (kahr-bah-oo)—The buffalo.

Kailassa (kye-lahs-sah)—A mountain in India.

Keromo (keh-ro-mo)—A man's name.

Koyo (koy-yo)—The name of a comic folklore hero.

Kris (kreess)—The dagger of unique design found in Indonesia.

Landak (lahn-dahk)—The porcupine.

Lombok (lohm-bohk)—One of the islands of Indonesia.

Lotong (lo-tong)—The monkey.

Macassar (mah-kahs-sahr)—A city of Celebes.

Mandau (mahn-dah-oo)—The name of a river.

Malay (mah-lay)—The name of the peninsula which forms the southeast tip of Asia, jutting into the South Pacific Ocean. Also the name of the people who reside there.

Malaya (mah-lay-ah)—The Malay Peninsula.

Malayu (mah-lye-oo)—The Malay language, spoken on the Peninsula and in Indonesia proper.

Machmud (mahk-mood)—A man's name.

Majapahit (mah-jah-pah-heet)—A Hindu dynasty in Indonesia before the rise of Islamic power.

Marapi (mah-rah-pee)—The name of a mountain.

Matjan (maht-jahn)—The tiger.

Mecca (mek-kah)—The birthplace of Mohammed in Arabia, to which Moslems make pilgrimages from all parts of the world.

Minangkabau (mee-nahng-kah-bah-oo)—The old name for West Sumatra.

Mohammed (moh-hahm-mehd)—The Prophet of the Moslem religion.

Moluccas (mo-luk-uz)—A group of islands in the Indonesian archipelago.

Moslem (mahz-lehm)—A follower of the religion of Mohammed.

Muntjak (moont-jahk)—The deer, also known as Manjangan and Rusa.

Nabaloi (nah-bah-loy)—The name given to a group of aboriginal people in the Philippines.

Negrito (neh-gree-toe)—The name of an aboriginal people spread through Oceania.

Oran (oh-rahn)—The word for man in Malayu.

Oran Badue (oh-rahn bah-dweh)—The name of a group of people living in western Java.

Oran Blanda (oh-rahn blahn-dah)—The Javanese name for the Dutch.

Oran Puti (oh-rahn poo-tee)—The Javanese name for the European, or white man.

Oran Tenger (oh-rahn tehn-gehr)—The Javanese name for mountain people.

Orangutan (oh-rahng-oo-tahn)—A species of ape inhabiting Southeast Asia and the Indonesian archipelago.

Padang (pah-dahng)—A city of Indonesia.

Pamudjo (pah-moo-djo)—A man's name.

Panchatantra (pahn-chah-tahn-trah)—A classic Indian collection of fables and folk tales.

Pantjak (pahnt-jahk)—An Indonesian wrestling sport.

Pelanduk (p'lahn-duck)—Another name for Kantchil the mouse deer.

Perak (peh-rahk)—An Indonesian town.

Pulag (poo-lahg)—A mountain in the Philippines.

Raja (rah-jah, or rah-yah)—King.

Rani (rah-nee)—Queen.

Ruteng (roo-tehng)—An Indonesian town.

Sadakah (sah-dah-kah)—An Indonesian custom of giving money gifts on special occasions.

Sanagara (sah-nah-gah-rah)—A Raja who once conquered a large part of Indonesia.

Sele basi (seh-leh bah-see)—In a dialect of Celebes, these words mean iron kris.

Singkarak (sing-kah-rahk)—The name of a lake.

Sumatra (soo-mah-trah)—One of the main islands of Indonesia.

Tjijak (tchee-jahk)—The lizard.

Tjik (tcheek)—The sound made by the lizard.

Tuan (twahn)—"Master," a term of respect.

Tuhan (too-hahn)—God.

Tuwan Benua Koling (too-wahn behn-oo-ah koh-ling)—A demigod.

This book may be kept

FOURTEEN DAYS

A fine of TWO CENTS will be charged
for each day the book is kept overtime.

JUL 1 7 '58		
AP 9 '58		
AUG 2 6 '80		
AUG 2 6 '60		
MAY 2 1 '66		
JA 9 '80		

Demco 291-B5